THE TOURNAMENT

THE TOURNAMENT

A Novel by
PETER VANSITTART

*Three masters ... Pain,
Time, and the royalty in the
Blood, Have taught me
Patience.*

SOPHOCLES

PETER OWEN · LONDON AND BOSTON

ISBN 0 7206 0616 0

Published 1984 by
PETER OWEN PUBLISHERS
73 Kenway Road London SW5 ORE and
99 Main Street Salem New Hampshire 03079

First published 1959 by The Bodley Head
© Peter Vansittart 1959

Printed in Great Britain by
St Edmundsbury Press Bury St Edmunds Suffolk

DEDICATED

WITH GRATITUDE AND RESPECT TO

J. Hampden Jackson

The starting-off impulse for this book was from a particularly evocative passage in Huizinga's fascinating and profound *The Waning of the Middle Ages* (Penguin: pp. 96–7). This later revived memories of Nöhl's extraordinary *The Black Death* (Allen & Unwin) read long ago in childhood. The quotations on pp. 32, 79, 203, 204 and 218 are from *Medieval Latin Lyrics* by kind permission of Helen Waddell and Messrs Constable Ltd.

P.V.

'Follow that Lord,
and look you mock him not.'

Hamlet

ONE

VALOUR was in the spring wind. Winter's white shabby
screens had been leaning anciently together across the
Duchy; to-day however the screens had toppled, revealing
green fields lost but now found, and trees already scattered
hard with bud, and a blue prodigal sky into which the
spires, towers, belfries soared more strongly than ever.
Already the winter 'He', disguised as a raven, had been
expelled from the hill-villages and, at the end of the week,
the leafed, green 'It', boy-beardless, would be riding his
ass into the capital, shining and heavy. People would hail
him with shouts and garlands, now that the sun was
healthy again and the three golden hairs had been restored
to the earth-giant.

The citizens were awake early. Rumours had grown
during the night and soon many figures were trudging
towards Mars Field, munching and spitting as they went.

'He's a devil, they say . . . a Red one. A Wanderer.
But our Duke will poke him for us.'

'Yet he's lusty. In bed. In saddle. Don't deny that.'

'Spy that.'

'Hush . . .'

'Our Duke is Saint Saturn of the Golden Age.'

Men-at-arms were already stationed round the damp
Field and the crowds did not care to advance too close.
Nevertheless, all could see the livery-men planting stakes,

7

gossiping, arguing while Maximilian Overseer rode to and fro with his attendants, making with his hands here an alley, there a tent, here the broad extended joust-plain itself while the onlookers, glad to be rid of rheumy winter, enchanted with this March radiance, alive with hopes and lusts, forgetting anxieties, chattered amongst themselves, and a beggar, known as the Pot on account of his inexhaustible greed, cried out:

'It's for all of us, friends . . . a great victory. They say . . . thousands.'

Crying and making clumsy dances he waved his cap until a baker-woman, irritable from having been bitten by a dog, threatened to beat him if he did not desist.

TWO

THE warmth did not penetrate the high stone council-room known as Perilous because of its height and the inaccessibility of the red and black ledges above the arches, beneath which, even in summer, mist seemed to hang, enlarging Perilous by reducing it to hints and vagueness.

Duke of Lancaster, the heavy central bell, had sounded eleven. The Lords of the Council, seated at a round table in the exact centre of the floor, paused, overwhelmed by the clangour which they pretended, nevertheless, not to notice. When this ceased the murmur persisted even here, from the powerful streets below, scarcely a bow-shot away. Around them, against the damp walls between bunches of blue hyssop and yellow verbena hung against sickness, were stretched tapestried hunting scenes, 'The Feast of the Ardennes', celebrating with oblique but discernible mockery that exploit of Duke Simon's grandfather, the first of the House, and whom it was now becoming safe to discuss, ghosts losing strength after the second generation.

Slightly faded, the light from the stained clerestory fell over them, picking out, then gently subduing with green, with purple, a caparisoned horse, a peaked subtle face, a hawk, before allowing them to relapse into the blur of the whole. At all times in Perilous candles must be lit and now, as the lords again raised their grave heads, their features seemed to waver as a draught caught the flames and, despite the gay notes of a chanson being plucked

9

without, they contracted, drew their furs closer, then frowned.

The Duke's throne, seven paces behind them, was empty, standing lonely in its cloth-of-gold and scarlet trimmings under an arch emblazoned with 'All Passes', the motto of the House. The table itself was not filled and the gaps further emphasised the gauntness, the councillors, each in his formal chair, often flanked by vacant seats, and speaking louder than usual with an effect of hollowness.

Present were the Lord Estrienne, Paymaster General and Sieur of the Bounty Magnificent: the Chevalier Stephen, the Duke's Noble Friend: Archbishop Jean Gaston La Borde: the High Chamberlain, Count Benedict: the secretary, Jew Plate. In and out of the dim arches, prowled Flavius the Nose, clustered with tiny bells. He was lean, beaked, observant, often pausing to smile, as if he could see what others could not.

Absent were the Chaplain and Huntsman, now attendant on the Duke, the Count of the March who had not been summoned, the Almoner who was, as he expressed it, on a pilgrimage, and the Grand Marshal, permanently indisposed following the jousting before Toul, though this could not be admitted.

Much of the business had already been completed. A humble though definite petition from the Vintners' Guild for the redress of the Battle Tax, the origins of which seemed to have been forgotten: an appeal from the Court of Requests: a routine complaint from the Lord Mayor and the Provost about the brawling and worse, to be expected on the Duke's return: the question of the interest on a loan, now due to the Messer Bardi: the riot at the maiming and hanging of thirteen rascals for an insult to the Trinity, a formality on which the Duke had particularly insisted.

'Her Highness the Duchess . . .', Jew Plate resumed. But there was silence. The Chevalier Stephen, tall and pink and awkward, stared moodily at the speaker and wondered yet again at the predicaments of a circumcised man and the love to be expected. 'Her Highness', the soft voice persisted, but it was from the arches that the first movement came as Flavius the Nose with his mottled dress, black and rose legs and sleeves, gaudy head-piece, emerged for a moment, showing side-glances and slanted smile and murmuring:

'He is crossing the floor towards the magnificent lords.'

The Archbishop spoke. A scholar, it was said of him that the vulgarity of its Greek always prevented him from reading the New Testament. Burly, robed in black and scarlet, with golden chain and crucifix, he wore his sleeves slatted with green in the fashionable Italian manner.

'Did not St. Thomas write, "Whatever is contrary to the natural order is vicious"?'

The faces continued, frowning and unsettled, streaked by the candle-lights, and it was the Lord Estrienne who suggested that the challenge should again be discussed.

He was dark and still sturdy with bright chilled eyes, short beard French-pointed, blue brittle nails. On all but Festivals he was never ashamed to wear the same clothes several days in succession, even in the presence of the Duke, to whom he had once been tutor. Unmarried, he was said to have connections with remnants of the Love-Haters of the South, who believed that only the pure should procreate. By his novel system of double-entry and his policies of extended credit he had aroused for himself the reputation of a wonder-worker, forcing money to breed wealth, not for himself, which was wonder enough, nor again for the Duke, who did not need it, but for the Duchy.

He now outlined, according to form, what the others already knew.

A year previously the Duke had celebrated the betrothal by proxy of his son, the Viscount Charles, to Isabel, Hereditary Countess of Trévers. At Candlemas last, however, the office of Imperial Estates at Innsbruck had been informed of the intended marriage of Isabel to Rainault, Prince of Utrecht, he whose mistress had been ordered by the Cardinal-Legate to do public penance for witch-craft. Such an insult involved the entire Duchy. The Duke had at once despatched Silver Herald with his mailed gauntlet to Rainault and now, for the Council's delibera-tion, the written Challenge had been prepared for the personal Combat between Duke and Prince, to save their people from bloodshed. Simultaneously a Universal Tournament had been promised for Midsummer Day, to honour the marriage of Isabel and Charles together with, it could be hoped, the downfall of Rainault.

'You will know, comprehend and realise', Count Benedict was tapping the thick layers of parchment, 'the completeness of the issue at Midsummer. Granted the favour, the dispensation, the strength and the liberality of our God and Seigneur, and of His Blessed Mother . . .'

Very tall and bald, with high forehead and wrinkled elegant face, furs knotted tight over the old-fashioned mail-coat he wore even in Council, Count Benedict had outwitted many devils and thus reached old age. How old he really was could not be ascertained for, by the hours spent at Mass throughout his life, by so much was his age shortened. He was a believer in Old Times, and his younger retainers complained that in his state-apartments he kept a stinking goat as a precaution against the Plague-Maiden and, during Lent, he ordered his females to sit naked and motionless for several hours a day, to tempt and frustrate the Perpetual Fiend. An authority on all manner of ceremony and degree, he found solace for any period of leisure in making a map of the extinct kingdom of Bevel. His favourite exclamation, frequently mocked, was, 'It is very extraordinary.'

In rusty, expressionless tones he began to read:

'To You who are the Most High, the Most Excellent Excellent, the Most Illustrious Rainault Raymond Michael Roger, Son Paramount of Christian, Prince of Utrecht, Lord Palatine of Récours, Holder in Fief Perpetual of the Baronies of Metz, Munch and Winchester, Advocate Supreme of Detmold, Lord of Marpat in fief to the Empire Most Holy, Most Roman and Most Exalted under God Sovereign and Saviour, You the said Rainault Raymond Michael Roger are summoned to appear Defendant in Arms on this Midsummer of Grace to meet, in all strength and purpose, and in respect of Her Serenity the Most Acknowledged and Mighty Isabel,

Countess of Trévers and Verdun, to meet, it is declared, Ourself, the Most High, the Most Noble, the Most Effulgent Simon, Chancellor and Commander of the Golden Ram, Lord of Meuse and Argonne, Vice-Trumpeter of the Eternal Empire, Keeper of the True and Only Faith, Chamberlain Exquisite of the Greeks, Baron Huntsman Glorious and Constable of the Rhine, President Given of the Joyous Entry of Brabant, Holder of the Cushion of the Wolf, Liegeman to our Lady of Dromme, Lord Marcher of Flanders, Bishop of Toul, Warden of Elp, Blessed Son of Saints Simon and Courtenay, Titular Earl of Kent and with the Reversion of Salisbury, Knight of the Fleece, Captain-General of the Seven Gifts, Knight of the Bath, We, Simon, the wilfully, wantonly and grievously insulted. . . .'

After he had concluded the heads inclined, finally bowed. The Chevalier Stephen murmured under his breath, and from the shadows sounded the thin stealthy bells of Flavius the Nose. Finally the Lord Estrienne, his cheeks now touched with a faint blue from the cold of the stone vault, remarked, 'Neither time nor purpose will transform Rainault. It was the poet out of Rome who noted that those who travel across seas change not themselves but only their skies.'

He smiled to himself. Within his words was a rebuff to the Noble Friend, himself a poet and voyager, of whom it was said amongst the people that he had lamed a knight by his satirical verses.

Soft, deferential, Jew Plate made reference to the resources, massivity and reputation of the Prince of Utrecht, adding that he was vassal to the Elector of Bavaria. Also that he was reputed to have a large liver and thus a powerful soul.

Rousing himself from private thoughts, the Archbishop said in his easy way, his remonstrance more formal than pointed, 'In the blessed words of Christ the Lord, Thou shalt not kill.'

The Lord Estrienne squeezed out another smile. 'It has always seemed to me disturbing, Your Grace, and also, perhaps, significant, that while we are permitted to hear the words of our Blessed Master, we shall never know the tone of voice in which he deigned to utter them.'

They were interrupted. A trumpet sounded from the Ardent Blue Court; Flavius started up, jingling and expectant, saying aloud, 'Now he hears the alarm.' And at once there came running in the Viscount Charles, flushed and hot even in this flimsy light.

The Duke's Heir was fully-grown, already a knight, golden-haired, with a beauty of limb and feature tainted only by the habitual ill-feeling on his mouth and eyes, and by the dark birth-mark, large as a rose-noble, on his left cheek, caused, some said, by the Duchess' bad dreams, though others, remembering his great-grandfather, gave a more sinister interpretation. Because of the disfigurement, the Court and people continually forgave him his outbursts and outrages.

He stood before the Council, panting, a quivering hound on his leash, a red surcoat about his shoulders. His voice unexpectedly swept into a shout at which Count Benedict shuddered and the Lord Estrienne looked impatient.

'Why was I not summoned? This is the Council. I am

my father's son. When there is no Duke then I am Duke. Why must I be insulted and scorned? Why?'

Behind him, miming his wild gestures, making antics, had crept Flavius the Nose, deftly avoiding the dangerous, suspicious hound. Reaching the Viscount's shoulder, dodging the blow that at once followed, he crowed invitingly, 'Of all men, fear thyself,' and darted away before he could be caught and thrashed.

All had pretended not to hear this last, and the Archbishop now said appeasingly: 'It was due neither to a wish to slander your Highness' exalted position nor to oversight, bane of councillors, nor yet again to our several inclinations and prejudices which are manifestly directed towards love of Your Highness, as in duty and reason born. But in accordance with our Lady Custom who decrees that the Throne shall not be filled except by Warrant Extraordinary from our Lord Duke, in this case neglected and indeed lacking. It would of course be unseemly and against prerogative for Your Highness to seat himself with his dutiful yet humble subjects, on a mean stool at the common table. And so we crave forgiveness.'

These words not only increased the youngster's agitation but renewed the interference of unseen Flavius who called out from far down the misty hall, 'Madness is his shield against devils.'

To notice Flavius would have been unseemly amongst lords but the golden Viscount stood staring, hating, yet bewildered, his blotched cheek even darker against the scarlet flush mounting on it. Then he uttered a harsh, even threatening laugh, a small greenish light in his eyes, before flinging out to rejoin his followers outside, the hound, released, speeding after him, yelping as he reached the sunlight.

The Chevalier Stephen spoke first, broodingly, as if to himself, staring at a candle-flame, momentarily tense and erect, 'There goes the last of the Dukes,' and the lords, avoiding each other's eyes, heard, like an echo, Flavius clapping hands, then dancing.

THREE

I<small>T</small> <small>WAS</small> the hour of Count Benedict. Ceremonies for the Duke's return were in his gift: he moved gravely through the day, commanding, urging, reproving, accompanied by a Vice-Chamberlain or Jew Plate.

The Count was unmarried, though he had a son who had died at twelve, fighting the English, to his father's pride. Once he had been betrothed to Eloise of Toulouse, whom he had never seen, but the dowry had proved inadequate and when the betrothal had been annulled on grounds that the two had been baptised by the same Bishop, young Benedict had turned with relief to chastity and battles. Now he was old but there remained much to remember, much to oversee, much to do.

There was the Chapel-Master to be asked to rehearse the boys in a more seemly manner: the Chevalier Stephen must inspect the *Welcome* Chansonette written by a new poet from Flanders: arrangements must be made for Flavius the Nose to be struck on the face three times with willow wands, by a virgin, could one be found: the Lord Estrienne must be consulted about payments overdue to the Scottish Order: and alterations be completed in the Duchess' bedchamber, there being estrangement between her and the Duke.

Furthermore, a new wing had been commanded for the Countess Isabel, and a message must be drafted at once to the Estates, who had already voted a set of gold for Her Serenity, perhaps conceiving that this voluntary act might excuse them from contributing further. They must

18

be reminded that the wealth of the Northern Provinces was greater than ever, with bales, barrels and monies on every side.

The Countess was four years older than young Charles, who had for weeks been agitating for at least a painting of his beloved. Voices intoned her praises daily: she was as dark as a raven's wing, slender as a lance, virgin as Dian or snow: she had eyes like the sky, like April, like Vivien's pools, a neck like a swan's. It was also true that none of the courtiers had ever seen her, and the Viscount would not be appeased. With angry violence he abused his chaplain, his chancellor, Count Benedict himself, storming that men were in league with that marauder Rainault and hiding away Isabel for themselves.

In the capital, high collection of red belfries, spires, pillared guildhalls, of quays and warehouses, arcades and canals and yards, the arches were rising, bannerets being prepared, while the unmarried settled down to make garlands of spring leaves. A new bridge had been built over the river, a league from the walls, to bear the processions, and a live child had been sunk in the water to give spirit to the bridge. Rivers, it was known, hated bridges and would destroy them if possible, though this must not be said aloud.

Prayers sounded on all sides that the unexpected and auspicious sunlight might continue. At Court between dances, while Count Benedict continued his peregrinations and the boys' voices rose clear and unmottled, parallel to the grey vaulted stone, and the Chapel-Master conducted himself with more restraint, while the prayers droned from side-chapels and ladies pattered to confession

and, in the nine kitchens, maidservants played monk-
and-run with the archers, the lords repeated to each other
the story of the goose-girl of Pszytullen, the only survivor
God had allowed from the black Plague in those parts and
who, arrayed in the jewels and dresses of her dead
mistress, had sat enthroned in sullen, forsaken grandeur.
It was a tale that the Duke particularly liked to hear, and
must be told him again on his return.

Flavius the Nose, having received his blows, was in
distinct fettle, beating his rival, Hode Hunchback, and
making ribald remarks about Prince Rainault's mistress,
she of the fair locks and, it was said, blue lips. Flavius'
own wife was too tall and he was always devising new
ways to shorten her.

Avoiding Count Benedict, he was discussing the monks
of Castleheim with whom he had been bargaining for a
consignment of aphrodisiac pictures. 'Lustful old cocks,'
he had said, 'they stew away. They stew. In stews. He
knows.'

The paintings were passed as eagerly as was considered
courtly from hand to hand, grossness in such matters
being known to protect you from those wiles that were
unseen.

The atmosphere was nervy. Shaky Abbot Martin,
though he had long since lost his abbey and was so old
that he could remember the Duke's grandfather, he who
had fattened dwarfs and infants into the shapes of mugs
and barrels, tottered about under the tired smiles and
faint laughs of the courtiers, mumbling that the Duke
was never allowed to wear knots, though only the very
wise, the very foolish or the very old could now under-

stand why. And Viscount Charles, playing cup-and-ball, without warning, assaulted Young Roger, his favourite page and bedfellow, kicking out two teeth.

Meeting the Archbishop after Mass, Count Benedict paused to shake his head, then helped himself to sugared capon offered by stewards kneeling on white mats. He ate wryly, for it was still the time of Lent.

'You oppose our Tournament, Your Grace, even though the Duke himself . . . but did not David challenge the Lord Giant of Gath?'

The Archbishop made his grave, deliberate gesture. His voice moderate, flavoured with too much holy oil, said the esquires. 'God is indeed Love but the world in its violence has become evil. Satan disturbs God's work. We are fallen angels, imprisoned in flesh, in matter, in the lordships of this world. It is permitted to fight only if, in so doing, we fight in order to chastise ourselves. We must struggle back to the light. Our Lord Duke . . .'

The two ageing men stopped as Jew Plate trod softly past and those who had been listening in alcoves, exchanged amused smiles. Reproving the stewards and their profane meat the Archbishop said conventionally:

'Sin waiteth at the Gate, and Sin lieth at the Door.'

FOUR

WATCHED by its young ghost, the river flowed peaceably beneath the new bridge, itself arched and festooned. Naked girls dived and breasted the water, naiads to welcome their god's return. There had been a storm in the night but now the broad clouds were white and empty, upheld in sunlight, assuming random but propitious shapes in the breeze.

The crowds now stretched from the walls of the older city to the river, smiling and laughing under the soft sky, crowds on battlements, crowds in markets and over gates, crowds packing the high road while hucksters cried fish, fruit and wonders, and thieves thrived and children danced with invisible companions, laughing at the lunatics and God-touched chained to the roofs among slanted, drying logs; throwing wintered apples at women, chasing dogs.

You can tell a city's wealth by the number of its chimneys; and here there were long acres of them, painted and beflagged, watched over by the spirits of saints. Colour was everywhere: in the women's red and yellow kerchiefs, in the tall straw hats of virgins and would-be virgins, in the scarlet leggings of ducal attendants as they rode importantly up and down the road, in the children's hoods, in the stoles, in the florid jerkins and black and peach bannerets, and the grasses and maypoles and striped arches, the very atmosphere tinted, to remind the devout that God had let Spring wander before her time.

Already, cap in hand, the bands of citizens were awaiting the processions. These promised to be even better
than the execution of Master Saint Ducher last month,
which had lasted two hours. Bagpipes were wailing, hands
were being clapped and from under the Philip Gate
drunken voices were intoning:

> 'Monks, parsons and chemists,
> Dentists and shavers,
> Quacks and greasers and all sorts of bathers,
> Jews, and with wisdom ninefold-endowed wives,
> They cure with rubbish all the ills of our lives.'

Beacons had been lit on the low surrounding hills and
on the walls of distant castles, flickering palely in the
sunlight like the Forlorn Fires burned by those who had
been enchanted; and in the fields, behind the gesticulating
mobs, garlands had even been placed on those sheep's
skulls stuck on poles to protect the land against lightning.
It was also said that the young people had swarmed the
woods and slain a wren that wore a golden crown.

Voices were rising rapidly, becoming shouts:

'My wife's called Chicken Tongue. She's a chicken in
bed and a tongue all the rest of the time.'

'They say our good Duchess has it again. A little
ninny in her pot, God bless on her loving ways. God's
doing.'

'Only a dawcock would believe that.'

'Who are you calling cock?'

'They say that the Duke . . .'

'Don't say it, brother . . . say nothing. . . .'

A friar went by, mumbling for alms and winking at

women. The packed crowd gathered closer, peering down
the road. At the back a gang of University students on
carts were arguing about Sir Plato and the 'Only Good',
to which a broken knight, his breeches faded and his
breast-plate long out of fashion, listened with anger and
frustration. Old men were hobbling towards the river to
spy the naiads.

The first cheers arose when Viscount Charles rode past
headlong followed by his chosen squires, the Wild Boars,
pledged to follow him even to madness and hell. In blue
and silver, scarlet plumes and sashes streaming behind
them, they fled through dust and sunlight to greet the
Duke, citizens waving and bawling as they went.

At noon, from Cathedral, guildhalls, churches, monasteries the bells were clanging, resounding: Gay Marion,
Blithe Robin, Wild Tom, Saint Hilaire, Saint James,
Saint Felix, Harn the Martyr, Susannah-Broad-in-the-
Girth . . . and the new Augsburg cannon banged from
the walls, making many cross themselves and whisper
about infernal shadows, Thor's mark and a curse from
Old Times. Then, out of the rolling dust the procession
could be seen, approaching the city.

Huntsmen came first, riding silken gennets and blowing
silver trumpets an ell long, followed by soldiers in black
spotted with red rosettes, then ladies of the Duchess'
Household, all tassels and hennins, with tiny flags tied
to their pages' lances. A short interval was broken by
the Knights of the Green Mask on immense pacing horses.
After them, more slowly, the tableaux: the Court of
Bulgaria on the back of an elephant, purple and staring,
waxed idols, but so lifelike that the children retreated in

dismay and were cuffed for treading on their elders' feet:
also walking windmills twenty feet high: a naked girl on
a golden platform borne by giants, representing the
Virgin Duchy: the Giant of Cornwall, one-eyed with
ferocious knotted club: dancing goats led on silver
strings: Caesar, Lord of France, and Pompey his ape.
Then the Kings-of-Chance throwing silver and bowing,
their faces set and stern. Marching in step, beating gongs,
heavy, solid, visored, glinting with metal, strode the
men-at-arms, escorting the Standard Bearer and his
herald bearing the immense unfurled banner with its
marigolds and fleeces, its leopards and lyre, all converging
on the White Stag of the House. Kings-of-Arms with
flashing swords and stiff bannerets preceded Hannibal,
Armadis of Gaul, Roland of the Household, Lady Helen
and Knight Scipio. Another interval, then a camel
covered with damask and led by a turbaned Saracen:
after them the Guild of Notaries with their ebony crucifix: the Doctors and Chancellors of the University
flanked by chanting choirs: the Architect General and
his retinue all in white: the scarlet Lord Magistrates, the
Venetian clarissimoes, the Spanish and Bavarian Legers,
the Lord Tributaries, the ambassadors from the rival
English courts eying each other with unpleasant expressions, their gilded followers already brawling: the heads
of the Estates General trooping after an immense bale of
wool. The Embassy of France: the Divine Manifesto of
the Empire: the Captain Registrar with his jewelled mace,
the Marshal of Nobility surrounded by pages in golden
armour: the Grand Huntsman with the hounds wearing
black and silver leggings and diminutive green helmets.

The Master of the Unicorns in white and a stiff peaked
cap surmounted by a god in ecstacy. The Prior of St.
Martin, the Canons of the Chapter and their Dean. Brown
and yellow men-at-arms with their halberds hoisted: Scots
mercenaries in grey and green: the ducal leopards, sinuous
and padded, snuffing from one side to another, applauded
highly by those who tossed them bones, filth, dried figs,
especially the children who danced higher than ever and
were often beaten by their fathers as a reward. Shining
retainers passed almost stealthily with hawks on their
wrists, belted and hooded: a band of trumpeters, pipers
and knuckle-drummers: a grey company of friars hooted
at and pelted with whatever could be found: a Chamberlain in red, with a stiff yellow plume as tall as himself,
bearing a motley cloak on a golden tray, another carrying
the Mirrors, a third with parchments, a fourth, the Herald
Extraordinary, tossing a golden lantern. Then more
priests, the monks of Bethlehem walking raggedly and
with bowed heads, one holding an ivory crucifix of
towering height. Immediately after them were two
bishops, jewelled, coped, mitred: the Sword, the Lord
of the World, held erect by a giant: a beaked and hooded
figure on stilts; then, side by side, on glittering horses,
like effigies, exchanging no words, the Duke and Duchess,
looking neither to left nor right, with dwarfs and the
smallest possible pages below them tossing coins from
trays, and with the Heir and his Boars following, more
calmly than usual. After them ranged the crested,
armoured lords and ladies on palfreys splendid with
ostrich feathers: also the Provost, the Lord Mayor,
sabled, gold-chained merchants and consuls: the small

scarlet figure of the Cardinal-Legate amid boys in green bearing willow wands. And the Grand Almoner, the Master of the Horse, the Count of the Liveries, the Sergeant of the Armouries. Then a quarter-mile of the Duke's baggage wagons, windows, casks. A White Stag of painted alabaster. Particular interest and awe was provoked by the guns, the Lady of Liège, the Midwife of Sorrows, Clacking Thomas, Vulcan's Cock, Master Jacques' Tool, the Cloud and the Fire, the Apostle of Wrath . . . slender and chased and wheeled, chaste, *not yet speaking*, forever on the verge, moving forward with terrible reticence while people knelt, crossed themselves, whispered about the Turk, the Duke's grandfather, the alchemist Helmstatter, and much else that should be kept silent.

Mirth was restored by the clowns, Hode Hunchback prancing on a piebald stallion, Flavius the Nose in a creaking stately coach blessing the mocking crowds as he passed, bare-headed in imitation of the Duke. Before long came the menagerie: ostriches led by dark-skinned boys on ponies, more camels burdened with thick coloured bales, a crocodile asleep in a tank, the ape Hercules, a panther held on silver strings by grinning Nubians. There also marched the Surgeons, the Lord Surveyor, the Abbot of Lint. Also a litter containing the Relics. At Saint Orpheus, within the sight of the walls, boys were being stripped and beaten with alder rods, so that their tears would fertilise the soil.

None could guess the Duke's mood. Still slim, with a blue cloak slung sternly over his hauberk, his face with its dark brown, ungiving eyes, and mouth sheafed by the short pointed beard, revealed nothing. He bestrode the brocaded horse, enclosed, as though intent on secret voices, the shouting crowds leagues away and his capital forgotten.

The walls were thronged. Flags, blazons, arches soared above vivid blocks of applauding citizens. Archers were waving arblasts, a butcher had hoisted aloft a thick haunch of venison. Ladies in blue and red tippets were raining down fresh leaves beneath banners several yards wide, all greens and violets, the Duchess' colours. For her the University scholars gave a special cheer, not only on account of her name, Katherine, but because of her graciousness and beauty. Waiting, was an exhibition of goblets, telescopes and mirrors prepared by the Followers of the Mystery of Glass, and a tableau of the Flight into Egypt, arranged by the Clothiers' Guild.

Streets were muddy, stirred up by the night's rain and thousands of excited feet. In the Jews' Market some cattle were already being roasted and ill-wishers defiantly brandished lumps of pork. Horn windows and glass windows alike were mired and bespattered. Bells pealed on all sides.

The cavalcade was now mounting the Street of the Three Kings, people jamming roofs, balconies, alleys to cry and wave and dance, when unexpectedly the Duke drew rein. Slowly the entire file, glistening and stiff, halted. Everyone stared, the bells clanging in air suddenly emptied of voices, their clamour magnified, filling the sky. In a pool, under an ancient stone cross, clad in dirty sacking, his face gaunt and burning, a decrepit beggar was standing, gazing through vast parched eyes at the procession, as though about to curse.

Deliberately the Duke dismounted: his black pointed shoes with their steel coverlets and rubied buckles sank into the liquid mud. All had perforce to follow, the Duchess and her courtiers, the Cardinal-Legate, the ambassadors, joining the barefooted friars and destroying their fine shoes for ever. Already, pages were kneeling in the pool, shaking the last coins over the beggar's feet. Only Flavius the Nose remained smug and secure in his coach although, as the crowd recovered, he had to dodge the mud flung in on him by indignant children and women.

The Duke stood with a malicious smile, one hand on his horse's mane, the Duchess standing slightly behind, sunlight falling over her pearled, black satin wrists, her high embusked breasts, shining on her bare temples and high forehead under the green conical hennin. Further apart Viscount Charles, frowning and muttering, the blotch on his cheek glaring more than ever, as it always did when he was angry. At his elbow was Young Roger, together with the Yellow Warrant Guardian of the Court of Requests.

Something of the elation had gone and would not be recovered. The elephant, the giants, the man on stilts had vanished: the tumblers were sulky and the musicians silent. As the processions resumed, under the gabled roofs, soaring towers and belfries, under Cathedral spires and arcaded galleries of the merchants, under the inescapable cross of Saint Hilaire and the Cloth Market belfry, the gongs sounded dismal and at last, looking up, the thousands of eyes saw that the sky had become tribulation-grey. Soon the sun would be exiled, and

29

already there could be heard shouts and threats as porters, retainers and goldsmiths swarmed to the attack, fighting for the right of laying purple over the stones before the Arch of John the Good.

FIVE

THE DUCHY, with its team of captured provinces, lacked natural frontiers. All crossed it: a fleeing King of Cyprus: lugubrious files of flagellants, each man beating the naked back before him and droning for the Lord's mercy: a delegation from the King of the Romans: Secrets from Flanders: pipers promising to make all men whole: Free Companies from the Confederation or from Modena or Parma, offering spears to the marcherlords: fashions from Venice and Genoa, Florence and Palermo: talk of old Nostradamus and his round world and his prophecy of a tragedy at Varennes: a new tune for viol or virginal. Rumours too: that an arm of St. George had fallen from heaven upon the altar of St. Pantaleon at Cologne, that the Turks were moving again, that a mermaid had been washed up on the shores of Friesland, that the University of Salerno had cut open a Moor to prove that an infidel could possess no soul. There was also a rumour that the Plague Maiden in black smock and gripping a red banner had been stalking the Rhine carrying in her armpit a new sickness that would kill men as they loved: but of that, a hideous scar on the smiling features of this new year, one would not speak.

Amongst older folk some misgiving had been roused at the fashion for the abominable heathen gods. About Court young men were finding it fashionable to swear by Bacchus and Diana while, in a park, in a grove there now glimmered Prince Phoebus in his nakedness, or the impure Lady Venus to tempt men to her Holda-hell, as though the Flight into Egypt or the Angel at the Tomb had never been. Finding much amiss in castles and palaces, the pious grumbled amongst themselves, not always softly, despite the Pope's pronouncement that pleasure was necessary for the preservation of man. At Windlesheim, moreover, the monks had set up a statue of old Priapus to succour cattle from blain.

Particularly favouring the new ways was the Chevalier Stephen who, in his craving for joy and metres, had been compared to Dominie Budaeus, so engrossed in his books that he forgot his own wedding day. The Chevalier himself was married but chaste: as the Duke's Noble Friend he was of course dedicated to the Duchess, for whom he made verses on ceremonial occasions. His own wife reclined in the country amid parrots and flowers, dangling between elegant fingers the Chevalier's latest verses, which she could not understand, or his new translation from the relics of Benedictbeurn:

'With glory of the goddess
    Are the old legends full,
Of Daphne and Apollo
    Europa and the Bull
        Aves nunc in silva canunt.'

Greybeards whispered more aggrievedly than ever and leaned together with long mournful expressions. What was wrong with St. Jerome in his wilderness, the stricken weeping Virgin, the Master of Pity and Suffering pierced by vile Longus' spear? Clearly, Lot's landscape lay ahead for this sinful age, so obsessed with gold and song, with tournaments and long pointed shoes.

32

Though the Cardinal-Legate had not spoken, it was known that the Archbishop had warned the Duke against the Midsummer Tournament, reminding him that the Church enjoined against such unprofitable diversions, not on account of their violence, for had we not been bidden to take up arms against Satan, but because of the lascivious thoughts they engendered, particularly amongst the poorer brethren. The Duke had frowned, quoted Origen, quoted indeed Augustine, ordered the challenge to be confirmed but had the Chapel Royal filled with penitential violets.

Much abuse was thrown against Rainault of Utrecht, as if he were a Wild Man. The marriage of Isabel to Charles was popular, 'for when our lords have wives the corn ripens'. Midsummer, furthermore, was the Duke's day: when the sun was in highest splendour the Duke, sun of his people, was full lord of the land and would therefore be at his most virile. His son also, people said, winking.

As the evenings continued fine, blossom already hanging like dark lace against the dying sky, many found themselves flocking towards Mars Field, after work, to see what preparations were yet forward. The Fountain was not yet wrought though its site had been christened, and already the Pavilion was rising in which Isabel, or an effigy of Isabel would be placed, Lady of the Tournament, holding the unicorn decorated with three shields. Following the Combat between Duke Simon and Prince Rainault would be the Unicorn Tournament, and on the first day of the three months preceding, the knights would ride in to touch the shields, pledging themselves.

Everyone was speculating about the Countess Isabel and promising each other a summer of adventure and beauty. Though the Duke's talk of a Crusade had momentarily vanished, the Combat would be fair recompense and less generally fatiguing. Furthermore, starting the Gallant Season, All Fools' Day was at hand and to-morrow the priests would be swung on high to ensure the harvest.

SIX

On All Fools' Day the Court rose early with prayers to St. Hilaire and the Blessed Stercutius and Cloacina, Lords of Privies. Down in the city the children had long been astir, being despatched by their fathers to fetch a cut on the rump or a bucket of stallion's milk. Soon voices were breaking out into old tales, old wonders.

'Hey Mother, remember . . . we could kill the sun.'

'Eh now . . .'

'By wounding it in the heel. To-day. Like the Snake biting old Adam.'

In the Palace horns and viols, trumpets and pipes had been sounding since dawn. Greeting each other in the Hall of Lesser Gold, that of the Lady in Arms, the noblemen eyed the others' garments, alert for any ring, jewel, ornament that might have been forgotten and therefore claimed as forfeit. But when the trumpets sounded Robin's Call, all vanished, to reappear dressed meanly and dirtily. The Chevalier Stephen was in sackcloth with long grimed legs and his bright hair dusty : Count Benedict was in a coarse Capuchin gown : the Lord Estrienne was even blacker than usual. Ladies were in serving smocks, one breast bare and dirtied; and without shoes. Under tapestries of Prince Hercules and his Labours, the serving-men stood aglow in their lords' costumes. Also heralds with their tabards reversed, and the dwarfs in gold and finery.

Above the Arch of the Fearless generally stood a painted image of the Virgin, jewel-crusty, the belly of

which would open to reveal the merciful Christ-child;
to-day, however, it had been replaced by the grinning
figure of Holy Saint Joseph, the Great Fool.

A cry of dissent, noisy but trained, greeted the Duke.
No trumpets had preceded him but suddenly he was seen,
in pure saffron with a red peaked cap and pearled collar.
Courtiers shook their heads and turned their backs:
several servants passed him disdainfully, without
obeisances, and the Duchess, in rags and rents, crossed
his path as if she did not see him.

Naked but for a cloth, Hode Hunchback crawled up
to him, Hode, of whom it was said in the kitchens that
he could lay eggs and was descended from a stoat.

'Sir Duke Man . . . I have duty.'

'I grant it. Beseeching mercy.'

The Duke's voice was quiet, slightly tired even at this
hour.

'Sir Duke Man. Treasure waits for you in the Arbour
Foix.'

'Name it. Beseeching mercy. Who gives it?'

The hunchback, not a dwarf but short and thick-set
with a seamed angry face, grinned. 'From Eve's mother.
Who else!'

The Duke shrugged, then turning, left the room
followed by Hode, strutting now and without his usual
caution, showing a tongue at Flavius the Nose as he
passed. At once the talk resumed, general liveliness
asserted itself, lords drew bladders and struck ladies'
buttocks, loudly making evening assignments with anyone but their wives, dancing peasant measures in time to
crude pipes. After some time there was applause for a new

figure, in Archbishop's robes and mitre, carrying a crozier reversed and in his left hand. The fellow was Flavius and each man bowed, crossing himself contrariwise, then walking a few steps against the sun.

A sudden hush, then reverence. Hode had reappeared, clad now in the yellow, red and pearl, dragging after him the Duke, naked but for a kerchief at his sex. They moved together through lines of resplendent servitors and shabby courtiers to the small glimmering throne raised at the end of the hall under blue banners. After a long bow, the Duke helped Hode seat himself and, kneeling, was the first to pledge fealty, Hode, the Shadow Duke, lightly touching him with a white wand handed by lean, dirty Count Benedict. Led by the Lord Estrienne and the Noble Friend, the Court followed.

The Cathedral was crowded. The populace had swarmed in grabbing the favoured seats, noblemen and their ladies fitting in where they could. In the choir-stalls were ranged motley figures in donkeys' heads, now braying the hymn to Hilary, now praising the Holy Innocents, accompanying this with sinful and obscene signs. A high reredos had been built, displaying Pan ravishing a nymph.

Children were still climbing in and out of the Stalls of the Golden Ram, Stalls of the Knights Fleece, the Knights of the Sacred College, the Knights of the Seven Wounds. In mean seats or squatting on stones under the pillars was the main body of lords and retainers in sack-cloth and rags, many playing bale or eating tarts and siliberts. Kneeling outside the Grand Almoner's box, now occupied by five chained lunatics, sacred to Virgin and Moon, were Duke Simon and Duchess Katherine, wretchedly dressed, their heads sunk in their hands.

In the ducal stall under its quilted coverlets, amongst piled lilies, capered Hode, throwing out imaginary largesse, knighting the prettiest girls with flowers, dismissing the ill-favoured with scowls and obscenities, sometimes emitting a bray to rhyme with those from the choir.

Many were now dancing in the transepts, some waving strangled cats and dogs but, as the dances reached climax the organ thundered and at once the choir began bawling out in fierce disarray:

'My soul doth magnify the Evil and my spirit hath not
    rejoiced in God my saviour:
For Baal hath regarded the lower parts of his hand-
    maiden,
Behold from henceforth, all generations shall call me
    damned.
For he that is cursed hath touched me and blessed is
    his name.
And his kiss marks them that love him, throughout
    all generations.
God hath shown no strength in his arm, he hath not
    scattered the proud in the imagination of their
    hearts.
The mighty hath he not put down from their seat, nor
    hath he exalted the humble and meek.
He hath not filled the hungry with good things, nor
    hath he sent the rich empty away.
He, remembering his mercy, hath helped only his
    damned servant Jewry,

As he promised to their devils, Abraham and his seed
    for ever.
Hated be God the Father, Bastard and Holy Fiend,
As it never was in the beginning and never shall
    be.
Dark world, soon to end. Amen.'

As the chant ended, fists, stinking cats, fish were waved
and a few hurled at the kneeling, motionless Duke and
Duchess. Gusty laughter followed and drinks were
exchanged. Sitting with Young Roger under a torn
ancient flag, Charles muttered, 'Thalassocrat', with an
expression of puzzled wonder.

The Lord Estrienne robed in dusty black sat surrounded by young noblemen in jerkins and leather
breeches. His eyes moved from a goat that was urinating
over a chapel altar, then to the Hunchback Duke, all pomp
and grins in the carved ornate box surmounted by the
Great Sword and Banner of Our Most Ancient Duchy,
famous lords crouching at his feet.

In his caustic way the Lord Estrienne, covered by the
din, remarked to a slender begrimed youth: 'A circle can
be too complete. Remember, Jesus the Adon and Adept
thought it best to write only in the dust.'

Dressed as Archbishop, a choir-boy was praying aloud
for fornicators, pilgrims and swearers, sodomites and
friars, his fellows gesticulating uproariously, lined before
the mirthful lolling congregation. Then a rondel was
sung by nine countesses standing on the altar of Our
Lady the Virgin, bemoaning the seven sorrows of Venus
and extolling the twenty-one delights of her body until,
exhorted by bare capering urchins, glistening in an alb

PETER VANSITTART

of faithful-blue, Flavius the Nose was seen ascending the carved ancient pulpit.

Partial silence succeeded. Grey hordes craned forward eagerly, emitting a shout of merriment as he cocked a snook at the glaring Shadow Duke and, stabbing the air with an amice and lifting a painted hand, began solemnly:

'Listen, oh ye of no faith and much bastardy to the words and parables of Jesus, son of Miriam the Bethlehem hair-curler and her seducer, Joseph the Panther. "Ye shall love. It is permitted to love."'

Frantic clapping and calls. Flavius delicately poked his long thick nose. Then, as the noises subsided he hoisted his breeches meaningly and began again, leaning forward in the wavering light.

'Hear ye sinners, jabbers of other men's mares, ye great bellies and foolish minds. There were two Kings in the Island of Gloucester and Lancaster and York. They walked in the fields when the night stars were brighter than Bethlehem, House of the Bread. "See," says King Ninny, "my big field!" "Where is it?" says King Pebby. "Why," says Ninny, "what is the sky but my field?" "And in your turn do you see my herds ravaging your puny field?" "Where?" "Why, what are the stars but my sheep, and the moon is my golden drover." "But they are straying, you vaunting Pebby, I shall turn them off my field." "You shall not." "But I will."'

From the high shadowy pulpit Flavius' grin was wide and inviting. The masses below waited, suspended and staring.

'And they quarrelled until each King rushed to his town and gathered men and fought all over, slaying and

40

destroying. Finally Rhitta the Giant, Lord of Wales, aggrieved by such wildness, consulted his Laws, his greybeards and his Estates, then strode against those dream-Kings, beat them in lordly battlestorm and cut off their . . . beards.' Again Flavius winked: laughter welled up everywhere and the boys crowed. 'To revenge so vile and unseemly a disgrace the Twenty-Eight Lords of Britain swore to overcome that puny Rhitta, but lost, and were disbearded themselves, in the . . . South. "The foolish Kings Ninny and Pebby," says His Mightiness and Great Vigour, Rhitta of Wales, "had large fields as we have seen, yet how insignificant beside my own. I have a wide wide country, broader than Queen Bertha's foot. An immense realm is under my hand, under my knee, under my . . . law." Annoyed by such folly the Kings of Brittany, Ireland and the Islands gathered ships, fought Rhitta and were beaten. "See, my immense field, how fine it is, all the world under my hand, under my foot, under my . . . arse. I make my dung where I make it." And these Kings too lost their hairy beards and however angry they were they were lacking in potency. Then Giant Rhitta pointed to those goats Ninny and Pebby. "These foolish Things, these dreams, trespassed on each other's tiny fields and now they are but the beasts that wandered without leave into my vast and proper field, and I chased them out again, the Iscariots and sucklings. The oxen!" And it was at once whispered throughout that silly Island that they had indeed been changed into oxen. Rhitta made himself a great cloak from their beards and the women rushed to him, pullets that ye are, to rub themselves against it. It covered him

41

wholly, thus too did the women. Ye taps, ye drains, ye acorn-hunters. "And yet I have a thought that the collar chafes somewhat. I am told that Old Arthur has a fine beard, father of many beards, a lordship, a pumpship of a beard. Go, one of you trivialities, less than dust, and demand it of Master Arthur, under pain of duress and battle and terror." Thus said King Rhitta.'

Here many applauded, hissing Prince Rainault, and Hode bobbed up and down flourishing a halberd. Flavius frowned disdainfully. 'Master Arthur, the Old One, he who harried Hell and bore off the Cauldron, well, he was wrath and haughty, a man of mountains. The helmets of his knights shone like snow on the hill-tops. "It is a vile and evil message," says Master Arthur, "a message I despise, a message I trample on. Send me no such messages. As for my beard, friendly though it is and well trimmed for service it is by no means full grown, nor, when it is, will I surrender it to that cur Rhitta, who is no real lord but a boaster and trickster of mean account. Return and tell him that my beard, when extended, will poke him from his high stool and meanwhile his maggotty head is forfeit." Rhitta was very angry but,' Flavius raised his soft, glistening head, 'ye generation of vipers, his collar still chafes. Chafes still. Chafes.'

He stared down at them, then his vitality and memory suddenly drained out, he almost collapsed and, propped on the carved ancient ledge, whispered incoherently:

'He has said it. Worthy to be called thy son.'

The fairs were up in the streets. A horse's tail hanging from a wooden booth declared that Magister Veltmann had arrived, who could cure all dogs and horses from Ireland to the Golden Horn. To a tabor and cithern a bear was dancing on hot coals. Tipsters were foretelling a comet, dirty hands were displaying caged ospreys, trusses for the swag-bellied, unicorn horns to cure lecherous spots. Quacks sidled everywhere, offering aurum potabile against Death, though it was observed that they themselves were not young. Also on sale were fragments of the Nudiosi Stone which improved any eyes that watched them: salts against quinsy: rue for death-beds; fennel posies for the haggard Plague Maiden (where was she now?). Maimed children too were exhibited in low dark tents.

Other stalls were crowded with Barbary sugar, silver fibulars, Perin cakes, goats from Lorraine, plumbsticks, saveloys and powders for fire in which could be seen lizards and, by those with curdled souls, the Prince of Hell and his evil.

That night merrymaking would resound throughout the city: in the Palace, in the University Courts and the Guildhalls, in the Hôtel de Ville, in the markets and squares, baths and punch-houses. Jack O'Lent in his bourder hat would be pelted and already, with gasps and cries, lovers were coupling at the Sign of the Smock, and young Court dandies collecting in taverns about the University, youths who stimulated themselves by writing their lovers' names within their codpieces. Beggarly poets and scholars and the fresher whores were gathering for them. Drunkards scattered silver even to Saint Anthony's children, belled pigs that roamed the streets devouring offal and dung. Later, as the moon rose, the Wild Boars, Viscount Charles at their head, would sweep from the town to set alight a few farms.

In the Palace long trestle tables had been set in the Peers' Hall, piled with fruit, with cheeses, with bacon powdered and salted. Scullions and servers, grooms and kitchen wenches thronged the boards, Hode at the head of Table Premier, waited on by the Duke and Duchess and Count Benedict, while above in the galleries the minstrels plucked and bowed and the players gabbled and, dwarfed by the huge squared tapestries of Percival of Gaul, Youth and Sport, the Twelve Peers of France, all hazed and shaded and haunting as the candles dwindled in golden sockets, the courtiers hurried assiduously from the kitchen, still in rags and trundling in steaming platters and green flashing bottles.

As the shouts increased, much kissing was exchanged between the lords and the younger servants of both sexes: screams mingled with music, turning to jeers as the High Folk received gifts from their prancing drunken retainers. Countess Alain was ceremoniously proferred mistletoe to remedy her sterility: old Treasurer Bênoit received gloves for his wormy fingers. For Bishop Ton was a painting of Alexander, Father of Lies: for the Grand Almoner a pair of ram's horns, making everyone snigger: for Jew Plate a halter, amid groans. Hode, with vile grimaces, presented a dirty box to Flavius who, ordered by the Duke to open it, discovered a snake inside. Watched by all, the Duchess found, on a silver tray offered by kneeling huntsmen, a small ivory bed, empty. This provoked several spiteful whistles which were followed by an abrupt silence, even the musicians forgetting to continue.

Katherine's clear face with its blue, rather sad eyes, coloured, then went stiff. Count Benedict, old enough and agile in his ways, to be daring, said aloud, 'Whatever is said, she is our true Duchess.'

The Duke stared but made no reply. He was pale and far off, his mouth moody. He reached for a goblet and drank as if he did not realise that he was doing so.

The feast ended with dancing to honour Father Noah, the original fool: and the dancers of Kolbeck who cannot die because they desired to spend eternity in gambling. Massed forms now posed slowly through flaring torch-light, barely emerged from a dream, the consort moving in measured time as if to rhyme with distant stars. All dancers were disguised. Rags and cloths had been replaced by glimmering surcoats, slashed tights, high tiaras and jewelled caps. Many men wore visored masks of bulls' heads, boars' heads or the heads of emperors: their mistresses too were masked, to preserve decorum: they turned and paused exquisitely, nodding and inclining to the music, foins, purled skirts, emeralds passing between lights and shadows. Pages were everywhere, in purple and white, their hair frounced, or long and oiled, their hands white-gloved, holding caskets of baked warden-pears.

The atmosphere was moving easily, controlled by the deliberate music, itself issuing, the Chevalier Stephen had murmured, from the lights behind the universe: the lights in which true religion existed.

Hode had long been chased away; but Flavius the Nose

was bursting between the dancers, twirling alone, brandishing a silver ferrule. 'If words were woods there'd be many more fires.'

Everyone laughed, mouths swelling and stretching beneath masks. His pointed distorted face wrinkled up in delight, he waved the ferrule in three parallel slants, then lifted his head, the heavy nose seeming to snuff the music, with its winding lament and complaint and sorrow: his cheeks suddenly filled with holes and he chanted dismally: 'Were he to escape his folly he would to madness go.'

Many young men were formally in love with the Duchess and passed forward to kneel to her, as she sat in a smaller hall amongst her ladies, not dancing, for the Duke had no mind for it, or, as voices murmured, no mind for her. Presenting her with an ivory mirror-case the Chevalier Stephen, Noble Friend, had just fondled and kissed her naked breasts, 'Loving but not lusting, loving but revering my exalted Duchess.'

All were aware that the Duke's disposition was gloomy: he was now sitting aloof on his dais, where the torches had been sconced so that his face was almost invisible. Black bile in the ascendant. Rejecting attendance he sat erect and silent, his attitude averted, contemplating not the dancers but a tapestry of the Unicorn, lover of chastity. The night's later sports would not be for him, the courtiers realised uneasily: he would not be interested in seeing female dwarfs coupling with their mates, nor would he take his pleasure in taunting the blind, a sport particularly enjoyed by the Viscount Charles, who might at any moment return and thrust the evening to another plane.

The Lord Estrienne, despiser of dances yet unable to resist the analogies with which any spectacle immediately provided him, stood in shadows under a small purple dome, intent on the revolving figures, the varied tints and flames, the darting dwarfs, the frightened obsequious cripples who had now been dragged from their den to make sport: also the ladies on the dais opposite the Duke, with their tall hats, bright mantles, concealed faces. What jealousies, what agonies, what python desires bred and scuttled behind the masks?

His hand made a sudden movement, like a great moth awakened, and the graceful young minotaurs who had approached him caught the sharp edges of his smile and heard him say, 'The Naming of the Name . . . you comprehend?'

This made the youngsters turn back with rather wounded attitudes to the masks and cloaks and animal heads, so ragged by the baffling lights. Who was who? Almost, *what* was who? Each man had three names. His Real name, that which he wanted himself to be, the most vital part of himself, the origin of gods, the name he kept more secret than his sexual part. Lying on his pallet in the darkness, or in the mud and swamp of a castle dungeon, the merest Klaus or Jacques called himself Jesus, Alexander, Jove. A god too had always possessed his Real name, to surrender which would be to surrender his potency. The Real name was the soul: to entrust it to another would be to risk salvation, self-sufficiency. There was also the Nominal name, that which you actually were, could you but take the trouble to discover it. Thus Mars might in fact be Venus, Olympus might be Tartarus,

47

Innocent III might be Heinrich the Seventh, Mary might be Hecate.

Lastly was the Seeming name, that by which you were known, let it be Benedict, Rainault, Charles. The Duke was Seemingly Simon: Nominally, perhaps, Hermes: Really was he . . . and again the Lord Estrienne uncaged his small smile . . . Really was he Hercules, victor of tournaments?

Similarly, argued the Lord Estrienne, each man concealed his secret shape: lean ague-ridden Count Benedict was actually a warm sphere: the Grand Marshal, largest nobleman in the Duchy, actually had no shape at all; except Seemingly, did not even exist. The true use of language was neither for entertainment, nor again for song, but for the penetration of names, beside which, worship, praise, invocation were a misunderstanding and defilement of truth.

Here his thoughts were disturbed by a commotion at the end of the Hall. Damp and pale, his face unnaturally bare, a rider had hurried to the Duke and was already on his knees, striving to attract him. Abruptly the Duke arose, the music halted, all bowed, then, with a quick movement, with an impatience foreign to him, he jerked aside the fluted hangings and vanished.

At once everyone was nervy and astir and even the music could not revoke the changed atmosphere. Then a high voice flew out like a pennant and the chatter immediately drove out the Lord Estrienne to find meditation elsewhere.

'The painting has arrived . . . the painting . . . the Countess Isabel.'

SEVEN

THE Duke had once declared that all his days were the same, but never identical. It might be All-Hallows when, while the bells tolled and the people doffed, he would lay hands on his crown, proffered by the Archbishop and the Imperial Emissary. It might be May Day when he hunted in full ceremony, or Bel-Day when in November he stood in red before fires, or Corpus Christi when, in white, he accepted a missal from the University Chancellor.

The State Bed rose round him like a castle, protecting him with its heavy crimson curtains, its solid roof, its four posts sculptured with the grave, inviolable saints of the House, with their long swords and unflinching eyes. Everywhere there were woven the shields, crookedly embossed with the famed 'All Passes' that had scattered ducal families into all fields of Christendom. Along the window wall was a long seat of black marble backed by heads of gryphons and hydras: around were slender green and white cabinets: a black table covered with tall silver candlesticks topped with candles three feet high.

At seven the bells rolled and jangled and the Duke would pull the purple cord, parting the crimson walls. The silken page, already seated on the cushion below the bed, would start to read:

'Then said Aucassin, "Aged priests and old cripples and maimed folk go to heaven. But to hell will I go. For there travel the fair clerks and gracious knights slain in tournaments and high Wars: and the brave archers and

49

he who keeps his oath. And there go the fair courteous
ladies : and also the gold and silver, rich furs and minstrels,
and those who are happy in this wide world. With these
will I go, so only that I have Nicolette, my very sweet
friend, beside me." '

Sweet Nicolette, who raised her gown, displaying her
belly and restoring vigour to a sick pilgrim by the sight
of her dark rose.

The Duke lay in the early morning, listening, lying on
his right side according to duty and custom, his eyes half-
closed or, were it René reading, perhaps intent on that
pallid face, long straight hair: or on a particular flame in
the brazier now being brought in : on the sunlight re-
modelling a stone antler chiselled on the window-arch:
on the hard buttock of Saint Hubert, himself defying
left-handed demons at the end of the Bed.

Finally he would nod. The page vanished, leaving room
for a lord to enter and offer him the missal to kiss : then
a herald would slowly declare the Duke's title, then the
calendar day and its saint. Following him, Flavius the
Nose, not kneeling but aloof and sauntering, would hear
and interpret the Duke's dreams. Of a crowd of mourners
round a dying agonised hero who rips off a blazing shirt :
of temptation on a hill-top : of music as a god deserts a
city. Passing noblemen, priests, pages listened covertly,
for the Duke was suspected of inventing or inducing
certain of his dreams and sometimes hints of displeasure,
desire or policy seemed to lurk within. There had been
times when it was necessary to hand a pocket of crowns,
secretly, to Flavius, though his honesty was uncertain
and his indiscretions deliberate.

To-day there was nothing more ominous than a war-camp seen in a desert, a familiar tale which even the pages knew could mean no more than the Crusade on which the Duke was always intending to depart next year. Flavius gabbled off ejaculations about the Holy Sepulchre, in a perfunctory way, after which a bell rang. Rising naked from the wide scented mass of green sheets, purple cushions, the Duke stood silent while silent hands perfumed, shirted then robed him. Master Chalice knelt with the tray of sacred rings: White Agnes, the Ardent, Blue Islands, Faithful Lent, Blessed Mary, Mark of Moon, Jacob's Tear, and the rest.

The Duke selected, crossed himself, moved into the arbour so as to see himself in one of the long Italian mirrors he had made fashionable, despite their condemnation by the Chapter of Alne and the belief that sucking demons preyed within. Then he withdrew further, to the stool-room, where he remained reading his breviary for several minutes, before making way for Master Remy, so-called Count of the Island, whose gilded privilege it was to distribute the Duke's droppings to childless couples.

By the time that the Duke had received his confessor a short procession would have formed to escort him to the Octagon Chapel. Three times a week he would receive God, on other times listen to the singing, followed by a brief sermon from the Chaplain or visiting prelate. Last week a Flemish bishop had discussed whether all souls in Paradise were exactly thirty years old: and the Archdeacon of Meulleheim had recently maintained that the owl mentioned in the Book symbolised 'them', deliberately wrapping themselves in the gloom of Jewry.

Built into a painted wall as a protection against Time was the aged yet calm and smooth Apollo, that had soundlessly emerged from the earth years ago, and been placed here by the Duke's mother, to the scandal of various old men.

Drawing his mantle about him the Duke knelt on an onyx square, then prayed. An anthem was sung, extolling the wise company of angels that is both Three and Nine. Outside, under the long wall lined with tusked boar-heads, would be waiting the Grand Huntsman, holding the jewelled wine-bucket and ready for the day's orders. A new falconer had arrived from some German city and the Prince Designate of Leon had despatched a treatise on the flight of eagles.

Decorators, masons, secretaries too would be waiting, hoping that the Duke would notice them. Also Jew Plate with his book of Council Business, old Plate whose Latin was Valla-proof in its fluency.

To be invited to the Duke's breakfast was eagerly sought. At so fresh a time conversation was lively, favours were in the air, plans shone. Present this morning was the Chevalier Stephen, now bending to kiss the Duke's lustred hand. The Duke embraced him, as was fitting to a Noble Friend, though this he did without animation, like a tiring player.

The Chevalier was talkative. One of his young friends had completed a painting. This had already been con-demned in various quarters for its novelty.

'But what does it describe, my lord? In what way does it demoralise our people? Through the senses and affec-tions? By invoking the Evil Humour? By falsifying the

Laws? By contradicting the World or by agonising the sensibilities?'

The Chevalier pronged a fragment of pullet and gave his sweet, sleepy smile. 'He has painted four flowers, Your Grace, flowers from my own gardens. And these flowers show neither God's love nor the Virgin's chastity. They are neither the sighs of Venus nor the charms of immaturity. They are . . .' he paused invitingly, contemplating the roused suspended faces, 'they are flowers,' he concluded, pleased by their surprise and perplexity, 'naked flowers. Just flowers. Flowers.'

Later there might be a Council at which the Duke would preside, listening with grave immaculate features as disputes tilted this way and that. More trouble was brewing with the Lord Mayor and Commune : a delegation from the Signoria of Venice was suggesting that all Christian princes and states should agree on January as the prime month of the year. Problems had arisen about the imports of Pomeranian leather and an overdue consignment of Lombard armour. A Sienese mystic had written declaring that the Duke's life was threatened by an inauspicious conjunction of stars, advising him to retire to the Egyptian desert and refrain from arms and women. The English Pretender was demanding to be received and the Chandlers' Guild was proposing a Harvest Pageant. There were the usual complaints against friars. A message must be prepared for the Estates General, not at this moment sitting. A lazy mendicant was due to be tortured again by slitting and stones. The Body of a Holy Innocent was due to be kissed:

perhaps, it was cautiously suggested, Her Grace the Duchess might this time be besought.

Here the Duke seemed as if he had not heard, and the Council hastily moved to news of a famine near Ghent, caused apparently by the foul and impious language of priests and farmers.

There was also the question of a heresy charge, a baker having maintained that Adam and Eve had been the children of devils. At this the Duke looked irritated, Count Benedict worried, the Lord Estrienne amused and disposed to agree: until the Archbishop soothingly suggested that he should use the best of his poor and unworthy powers to placate the offended bishop and indignant archdeacon.

The Council proceeded. Between Habsburg and Capet must grow, like an oak divinely planted, the prosperity of our holy and magnificent Duchy.

Ceremoniously the Duke dismissed them. He would kiss his page of the day, then, preceded by the Wand Chamberlain without Garter, stride down the soundless tapestried passage towards the Duchess' new apartments. On the way under the Turkish grille, three kneeling merchants were anxious to sell the Duke a gold and ivory crucifix inscribed on the back with pictures of Apollo and Marsyas.

Beyond them, superintended by Guards, a row of poorer folk knelt for pardon for the condemned. To-day he might allow mercy: or had not enough people died lately, had there not been enough order and magnificence? Executions give rulers new strength.

The Duchess Katherine was awaiting him in the

Ochred Bedchamber. The Bed was already curtained, its plumed tassels hung motionless, flamed by the lancing sunlight, and Katherine stood on a low raised floor attended by her ladies.

Almost as tall as her lord, as slender as at their marriage, she was sheathed in dark-blue brocade, with both breasts covered, the stones at her neck flashing now green, now red, a tint of gold lurking in her black coiled hair. Her eyes, deep and blue, were quiet, prepared for him. At this moment two ladies were extending magnolia sprigs to her, the first of the year.

Entering alone, the Duke bowed three times, to which she severally inclined her head. His voice was measured, cold.

'It is impossible for my weak tongue to declare fully the depths of my pleasure in seeing how radiant and refreshed my Sister and Duchess is looking.'

Actually, Katherine appeared tired, even exhausted. The cheek beneath the wide full eye and shaven temple was faded and her bearing was too stiff. Now she smiled, looking past his head at the doorway draped with lilies and Hera-blue blossoms.

'I pray that God has allowed Your Grace a sweet and untroubled night.'

The Duke maintained himself, erect, twelve paces from the Duchess, on the lower floor. The ladies receded.

'Sorrow you as it may, I must inform you that I slept badly.'

'Why, my most gracious and loving lord?'

'For my love of you, for the memory of our past joys and the anticipation of our future delights,' the Duke

PETER VANSITTART

rejoined, 'but it rejoices me to see and declare the beauty of my most beloved, familiar and cherished wife. The beauty envied by the shades of African Dido, Helen of Phrygia, Eleanor Queen of the South and the impious Venus of Cyprus.'

They remained a few moments, exchanging conceits before he bowed and turned away, the curtains parting silently and as if without hands. At once the ladies crept back with their cool magnolias, now as though warding off from their mistress the invisible and malignant.

Soon she would be feeding the golden orfes in her pools. At noon, when the universe rested, the Noble Friend was to drink wine with her at the Trellise of Blanche in the Angevin Arbour, before she received the delegation from the Harp of Lorrant.

A new procession had formed outside. The Duke was led by the Keys, on a scarlet cushion. After him the precedence was strict, like a sequence of playing cards, like the holy stars. Count Benedict foremost, followed at seven paces by the Chaplain, then the Huntsman, the Master of the Wardrobe, the Emerald Seal, a Vice-Treasurer. To these, at nine paces, after the Silken Banner, attached himself Messer Floriano, master-sculptor, leading a commission of goldsmiths that bore, with hope for his purchase, a casket of golden roundels effigied with the Duke slaying a chimera.

Over them all chattered the voice, bells and laughter of Flavius the Nose. 'Did Christ wear clothes, for is not Truth naked?'

The Duke would inspect his animals, the hounds and horses, the elephant, the leopards and monkeys. He particularly enjoyed assisting at their feeding, fondling the heads, asking sharp questions, spending perhaps as long as an hour, talking familiarly with his favourite grooms and keepers, then, dismissing them, passing on to the falcon-house. Afterwards he re-entered the Palace. Trumpets sounded from four quarters and the wide doors opened to admit the Court.

The long ovalled hall was quickly flooded with advancing figures, a shining impression of long curled shoes, dainty eyes, jewelled chains, painted cheeks and beards, pyramidal head-dresses and coiffures, resplendent rings tricking the eye with all manner of fire.

Wine was poured, sweetmeats served, compliments recited, plans for the day discussed. Dogs with scented coats and rubied collars wandered about, nuzzling slim striped legs.

The Duke was suddenly gracious, toasting the ladies, presenting a necklace to a visiting Archduchess, jesting with the Regent Prior about Bran, a holy raven that had flown to the left. But before long Count Benedict was whispering to him. Already noon was approaching, when the Duke must stand rigid and unbreathing for a full moment.

A light meal was served for whoever of the Entry cared to attend. Mushrooms, carp, powdered bread, for it was still Lent. The Duke himself might be present, fondling his dogs, or sitting as if hearing nothing and repelling all, or perhaps starting and maintaining a discussion. In what manner and to what profundity had gods existed? Was there Law in heaven? Was fear of demons at the root of both laughter and marriage? Was Bettina

of Savoy the lover of Armand of Burgundy? Were pearls
the fragments of a vanished moon? Could one believe
that Saint Urge had hung his hat upon a sunbeam?

The Lord Estrienne was discussing the Bogomils who
apparently were Luciferians. God, he explained with
subdued, patient amusement, had had two sons: Satan
and Jesus. Satan, the elder, had been expelled for rebellious pride and had thereupon in pique created the
universe which was thus evil. Jesus had descended to
earth to earn a birthright and help doomed man, but had
failed.

'This makes great sense,' a young man declared,
glancing at the Duke's face, which expressed nothing.

The Archbishop, reaching for wine, smiled reprovingly.
'It makes great heresy, my son,' and drank with quiet
lingering pleasure.

'Mynheer Fugger was certainly not one of our lord's
successes,' interposed a third voice, rousing more smiles,
though these were still contained, poised to avert the
Duke's displeasure.

In the afternoon there might be hunting or tennis, or
the Duke might ride to the Halls of Justice or the Court
of Requests, either to deliver judgments or, from his
private gallery, to listen to the pleadings below, as
Master Fat-Span argued about degrees of Truth, and
Master Bulge bemoaned human cupidity, and the Archdeacon deplored curiosity, Satan's gift, and, above them
all, the scarlet judges with their heavy seasoned faces and
creaking manner gazed directly ahead, concealing singular
thoughts.

The Courts were always crowded, particularly in cold

weather. Almost always there was a show. Child Godfrey's father had in jest called him a killer, and to justify
the name and save his father from the sin of mendacity,
Godfrey had stabbed his sister. Peasant Mabot had been
sentenced to the gibbet for stealing a spade. He had
turned the spade into a hoe and could not be convinced
of the justice of his punishment. 'For,' he repeated
furiously, 'the masters have taken me on account of a
spade. But I have no spade. The spade has gone. There
is only a hoe, and the hoe is mine.' The Duke himself had
descended to reason with him but the old man only
shook his head surlily, complaining that he had been
notoriously and evilly wronged, so that in an effort to
convince him the hanging had been suspended, finally
cancelled, and Mabot had tramped away, demanding
compensation.

The Duke was known particularly to enjoy the early
evening. Returning from hunting, fencing or perhaps the
lists, he might, on dismounting, turn aside, whatever his
fatigue, to saunter in pleasaunces, seat himself by pools,
or contemplate the massive fountain that the Italian had
lately completed. Above bronze-coloured waters Actaeon,
already half a stag (the glittering marble mingling human
limbs with the forming antlers, and the anguished
entreating eye: animal, yet with the hot residue of
humanity still left in it), was writhing, screaming as his
own hounds leapt ferociously to tear him and, a few
yards away, rising from water, was Diana, naked, rigid
and relentless, the nymphs, half-immersed, crouching
white and frightened at her feet.

Again and again the Duke marvelled at the sculptor's

capture of that instant of transformation, Actaeon helpless, mid-way between man and beast, between stone and
life, between the limits of his own soul, so that the watcher
could scarcely see in leg, arm and face, claw and fang and
bristle, just where the one began and the other ended.
An exquisite analogy, the Chevalier Stephen had said, of
humanity blighted since Rome.

The Duke at last turned away, pages keeping their
distance. Impelled by the creeping shadows, birds were
whirring round a budding tree as if a dark giant were
twirling a many-coloured rope around him. Inspecting
the orrery, he listened as Messer Mario hurried forward
to explain the latest conjunctions, with a few compliments to the Duke as maintainer of stars and preserver of
the universe.

At supper after lauds the music played aloft, the ladies
sat at meat amid the scent of cloves. Several painters and
sculptors had been invited to the Duke's table where the
talk was vivid, lyrical, for the oil-paintings from the
Duchy were transforming even subtle Italy, from where
travellers, arriving daily, could talk of nothing but
Brunelleschi's dome. To-night a painter had brought a
triptych, worked in brilliant tints: Saint Joseph was
sawing logs, the Child, small and ugly, was grimacing
behind his mother's back while Saint John was sulkily
repairing trousers.

Excitedly, hands pointed at the triptych on its stand
before them.

'There it is: life . . . where's old Buoninsegna's
coffin . . . ?'

'Only the new and victorious could produce such

mastery. Now we can see how deep the Constantines are in the mud. They have lost their colour. They are ghosts.'

'Painting for the eye,' the Chevalier Stephen said, 'for the eye. For delight. Perhaps our painters are the first in the world who can trust their own eye. To paint without preaching. To paint.'

Before long the talk had climbed. Was it possible, the painters were asked, for a Christian to see merely the shape, the colour, the design in itself? For surely even a stone, even a drop of water carried a hint of God's plan and of its own celestial station? Moreover, and similarly, could one 'be' without 'doing'? And how far can you 'do' without spoiling your 'being'?

'There are people around,' Flavius the Nose said importantly, 'whom the ordinary man does not see.'

Later, each feaster might assume a character from antiquity, sustaining it throughout the evening, becoming the Stagirite, Kleomones the Liberator, the Lord Petronius, Plato the Wise, Martel the Conqueror, Nestor the Interminable, the ladies taking part as Poppaea, Sappho, the witch Medea, the Abbess Howistha, the Empress Theodora; then, when the Viscount Charles made a brief bullying appearance which nobody enjoyed, a voice murmured 'Catiline'.

White meat and wine were despatched to old Marc, who for thirty years had spent each day in day-long praying in a chantry for the Dukes. In the background music rose, fell: there was singing: toasts to each guest in turn, gold for the lolling smiling painters, a few routine words about the Holy Sepulchre, the need for a crusade and the preparations that were in hand both for this and for the famed Midsummer Tournament. To please the Duke, many jested about the coming doom of Prince Rainault, and some gave covert glances at the Viscount Charles.

The Heir was known to be angry with his father, vainly constraining him for a sight of that painting of the Countess Isabel which, all knew, His Grace was keeping in his private oratory, showing no-one. As always, the Duke's purposes were secret, not to be discussed.

To-night the Duke retired early, before the eunuch, Eneas Giorgione Cock, prowling the passages and vault, had crowed eleven. A rondel had been sung, praising the Duchess' beauty, Katherine herself being absent, after which the Duke stood up suddenly and, without bowing to the company and rejecting those who made to accompany him, strode to the gilded arch and was gone. Servants swiftly reported that he had made for his oratory, faster than was his habit.

As all the bells in the Duchy tolled midnight, Duke Simon, naked, alone in the wide curtained bed with a solitary taper burning, glanced again at the volume of Virgil sent him at Lammas by the Emperor.

'Unluckily he was felled by a wound not meant for him: and he looked at the sky and, dying, remembered the Argos that he had loved.'

EIGHT

A T the approach of Easter rain drew over the land, gently draping or obliterating whatever was definable, predictable, exact. Ramparts, turrets, gateways merged, becoming as it were, an unfinished whole. The Palace was hung with pasque-flowers: lilies and daffodils, wreaths and crosses of love-violet, crocus and White Banner.

Muddy, good-humoured people were crowding in from villages with willow-buds in their caps, waving branches that they were bringing to churches to be sprinkled with holy oil. Amongst the poorer classes expeditions were being planned to the hills to see the sun dance: a mock tourney was fought with narcissus-twined rods by the ducal dwarfs, and the Chevalier Stephen was teased by ladies for reminding them that, at Easter, the Lamb and the Flag were to be seen in the sun. Chapels were being draped in black for Good Friday. The powerful masons' and clothing guilds offered their yearly prizes for craft, drama, verse and the Disputes. It was said that the end of the world was almost due.

Further excitement was provoked when it became known that the embassy from that satyr and ill-begotten heretic Rainault had departed some days previously from Utrecht, bearing a reply to the Duke's challenge. Meanwhile the masons were levelling and hammering, plastering and digging, intoning secret passwords, exchanging esoteric hand-grips, and the foundations of the Countess Isabel's houseling were already laid. Above the noise, cheerful despite the wet, sounded the screams of a lady in labour, at which the lords shrugged and the servants winked, for who did not know that such pains were the penalty of Eve's sin?

The Lord Estrienne had laid aside his accounts and retired to a library. He had his own insights. Easter was the ancient time of the Hare: quivering, impulsive, as solitary yet as universal as a dream, which profoundly it was: immemorially a sacrifice to Mother and Virgin, as it sped across green it appeared to seek its own death in an effort to live more precariously.

The Embassy arrived on Palm Sunday. No Hosannah, but an unfamiliar and inescapable sound filled the streets before the first horses nosed round old Janus' gate, protector from witches. A measured beat as if from some hollow yet infernal heart, a gaunt echo for which there was as yet no word, primeval, from the breaking time of the world, and at which the citizens shuddered.

The Chevalier Stephen in carnation pink, watching from a balcony garlanded white and yellow for purity, felt his nerves quicken. Fine rain was falling about his long, brown, ribboned hair, making it a silky cowl. He murmured in delicious unease, 'In the glare of the Mongol shall no man live, neither shall the grass grow to tenderness. And the sun shall be hidden.'

Five Knights rode in, accompanied by close squads of foot-soldiers, trampling down the sodden wreaths and branches laid down to welcome the Saviour. Their casques, black, square and stilled, fitted entirely and their gorgets were thicker than a man's calves. A preying, bird-like appearance masked them. Their horses were

64

mantled in yellow, and yellow too were their shields, fierce and splenetic against sable armour. On a single baleful standard hung the Ram, Rainault's emblem, horned, tufted, motionless.

Within the tall yellowness, continuously beaten, round and immense, were the drums, hairy drums, Mongol drums, booming and humming throughout the city, slammed methodically long after the embassy had vanished, leaving behind awed faces that turned helplessly to each other for shelter.

The Knights appeared at court that evening, clanking in from out of the wet, men with raw scrubbed faces staring out from under pot-helm hair-trims. Their armour gleamed darkly beneath marty-red cloaks and their squires carried their helmets, plumed with that challenging yellow.

Stairs, balustrades, galleries were crowded and silenced. The Embassy was greeted by Chamberlain Mark, in silver breast armour and flaunting plumes, scarlet and blue. Accosted by the adamant forms, the noise of whose armour ripped open the silence as if with blades, several ladies crossed themselves. The iron, inauspicious Five rudely blocked the screens of daffodil and narcissus, the violet crocus and gentle saffron Christ. The dull ring of their feet would have become intolerable but for the dwarfs, painted white and gold, leaping and crawling and mocking them from behind, in a way that no sworn knight could seem to notice.

The Duke was stiff and pallid, enthroned, his face powdered so that any expression was extinct and only the fine tense bones and indifferent eyes remained. To

his right stood Count Benedict draped in a blue satin
gown and bearing the Shield. The dais was vested with
cloth of gold, and the immense grate behind, which had
once contained a manacled bear, was filled with mistletoe
and blossomy twigs of blackthorn and wild cherry.

The Knights halted in line under the dais. Their
herald, his tabard starred and quartered, stationed himself before them. From invisible apertures trumpets
sounded thrice. Chanted, the words rose as if to very God.

'We, Rainault Raymond Michael Roger, High Prince
of Utrecht, Baron Gallant of Metz and Munch and
Winchester, Lord of Marpat, do renounce and confront
and despise you who are Simon the Most Serene, Knight
of the Fleece, Lord of the Meuse and Argonne, Keeper
of the Faith, Grand Almoner of Provence, Comman-
dant and Suckler of the Wolf. Inasmuch as the said Lord
Duke has inspired, induced and imputed words and
insults most grievous, most condign and most evil
touching our honour, we, the Most High Rainault who
are Prince Purity of the Fountain of Liège, reject to your
teeth your pitiful and distressful abuse, and maintain on
oath and on pain of being declared Nothing, that we will
verily and indeed meet you in arms on the day coming of
Saint John the Blessed, in June Midsummer, trusting to
Lord God and his Angels, and more especially the Blessed
Warrior and Archangel Michael to defend the right. And
may the soul of he who retreats from this most solemn
and inspired Oath and Word be forfeit, spotted and
damned until the end of all.'

Again the trumpets brayed. Neither Duke nor Knights
made movement. Serried breathless faces around were

as if carved, and the spaces between figures suddenly emphatic and exact. Then, relapsing into easy tones, the herald explained that the lawyers of the universities of Paris and Utrecht, together with the Commissary of Navarre and the Magistri Concilium of Florence, had discovered a grammatical irregularity in the original marriage contract of their Highnesses Charles and Isabel, which was therefore null and void. Furthermore, the said contract had been drawn up under the Thirteenth Night of Orion, and therefore. . . .

The dwarfs were again throwing out ribald exchanges, pattering to and fro with expressions of importance, rolling their eyes, interfering with pantlers and stewards, kneeling in grotesque or obscene positions, and absurdly parodying the motionless Knights. Smiles were at last possible as Hode Hunchback stalked across the hall decorated with the arms of Prince Rainault and waving aloft a dried sheep. The White Stag would stick the Ram.

That night the Five were feasted by the Duke and his court, jealously watched by the hot eyes of Viscount Charles, raging less against the intruders than against his father who, as if taunting him, still concealed that portrait of Isabel. Like another Helen, Isabel was calling from across water, across hills, and from beyond. And, according to a tale told by the Noble Friend, it was only a false Helen who had wandered to Troy to trick and confuse, bringing about the fury of gods, while the true Helen stirred not and enjoyed the delights of love.

The feast was restrained. Even deep drinkers could still hear the low hiss and growls of the leopards in the

Hubertus Keep. And in the city no flagon was long enough to drown the pounding refrain of those drums, so loud even long after they had ceased: a foreboding not to be dissipated by loose talk of drumming one's wife or leman.

NINE

COUNT BENEDICT was often worried. Were the Five
Vices identical with the Seven Sins? Did cathedral spires
point the way to paradise or merely indicate the few
who were chosen? Was it not true that Saint John made
Christ say 'Touch Me Not', and Saint Luke, 'Handle
Me'? What too had happened to the Holy Crown of
Bevel?

Furthermore, the Viscount Charles would be the fourth
Duke: was this ominous or, in God's profound way,
propitious? In England the lords were tearing each other
to pieces, which showed fearsome disloyalty to lordship:
here at the Duke's court those graceless painters had
shown Judas not in the yellow of faithlessness but in
honest burgher costume. This too was a scandal.

The Count enjoyed standing in the small Courtyard of
the Unicorn. No unicorns had ever been seen there,
indeed it was known, despite the shining salaries of the
Master of the Unicorns, that they no longer existed, such
was the lustfulness of the times, and their passing—or
apparent passing—indicated the fading of the world itself.
Simultaneously it was agreed that, were a unicorn to
come, it would be to this shaded vine-clad yard.

This was one of a group, known as the Necklace, strung
between the Royal Wing and the Orangery, and the
Count had long been aware that if you waited in it long
enough someone would appear and make an interesting
remark.

Yesterday he had been standing absorbing the spring

sunlight, God's fresh mintage, and meditating on the word 'Ardent' . . . you burned, were even consumed, yet remained uninjured . . . and a strange monk, shorn in the manner of the House of Pavia, had spoken in a learned way about the library of the Grand Prince of Holland. Then, changing tone, he had repeated that disturbing belief that, were you to live beyond the age of eighty-four, God had no further interest in you, so that prayer was useless.

As it was never possible for a man to know his exact age this idea was discomforting. Of no less comfort was the Lord Estrienne's assurance that most of what passed for ideas did not exist. The Thing as it Is, he would repeat, with a small, suddenly bitter smile.

Count Benedict sighed. The times were frivolous, maladroit, clouded. In Spain the ecclesiastical office had condemned the Bible as being as heretical as the Koran. Various women were talking of nothing but the end of the world. Many of the common people were becoming so wealthy that they were attracted to lawlessness and oathbreaking.

Count Benedict lifted his grey bare head. No face could be seen at windows: the vine-buds glittered: birds rustled and sang. But he sighed again. The Duke was not interested in the making of new laws, had once indeed said in a moment of vexation that laws were all folly, though this had not prevented him from having ordered the hanging of a company of malefactors an hour later. But such a remark would have been unthinkable in the time of the old Duke and even that of the First, the Black One, who, though he indulged himself in abominations, had kept a strict view of what could be permitted to others. True, Council meetings were often lengthier, the deliberations of the Estates long-winded, pettifogging and at times impertinent: but if wise laws could not make people good or at least harmless, what could?

There was also the problem of the stews: last week two priests had been tracked there and the populace had not only murmured but laughed. Also, too much care was being taken about absurd and perhaps blasphemous fashion. Here at Court the Duchess of Flanders had stood upright all night on the eve of the Masque of Candles to avoid disturbing her hair-style, to the indignation of her husband.

All this frivolity when grave events were certainly at hand: Midsummer with its clash of arms, the Black Plague Maiden stalking the Rhine with wounded feet: and always God's mysteries. That uneasy verse in which it was written:

'There be some standing here which shall not taste of death till they see the Kingdom of God.'

The Cardinal-Legate was insufficiently learned and the Archbishop too preoccupied with the profanities of lascivious Ovid to probe such perplexities. Could it be that all was well with the noble and well-intentioned Duchy: or was the Duke to fight his Combat in an effort to avoid retribution?

The constraint between Duke and Duchess had not shifted: Katherine remained with her beauty, her ladies and admirers, cursed by Charles for not laying hands on that painting which only the Duke and his Confessor had yet seen.

Lent had passed : the Court had eaten the pie seven ells broad and stuffed with all manner of game. Now Easter was over. Adonis-gardens had vanished from the streets : man-high candles in the Cathedral had dwindled to nothing. Duke Simon had worn his crown. The Court had eaten the eggs boiled in green dye : between the suburbs the football, painted red or gold, had been kicked, to shouts of 'Gawain, Gawain'; and on the countryside the peasants had lamented, then leapt for 'Him'. Covered with waxen flowers dead Christ, Lord of the Vine, had been borne from Saint John's to the Cathedral by processions bearing crucifixes and tapers, the people wailing on their knees, as was seemly. At night the bells had jangled, the fires been waved, laughter flaunted, and many claimed to have heard 'summer music' in the hills. The Archbishop had declaimed old Abelard's verses :

> 'Solus ad victimam procedis, Domine
> Morti, te offerens quam Vénis tollere :'

to end triumphantly with :

> 'Sic praesens tridium in luctu ducere,
> Ut risum tribuas paschalis gratiae.'

Count Benedict shook his head. He was still alone. No interesting stranger had disturbed the ancient airs of the Unicorn Court. Nor must he linger. Matters must be strictly attended to. Hours were passing. He had sent for Rainault's horoscope but it had not yet arrived. In appearance, the Prince's record was dismaying : Lord of the Lists at Montpelier, of Strasbourg, Knight-Victor of Palermo, Champion at Châlons : Mailed Service with the King of the Romans, the Dedicated of Castille, the

Knights of Calatrava. To throw down such a paladin a dexterous physique was almost as necessary as prayer.

Fortunately Duke Simon was stirring himself, laying aside the volumes sent by the Queen of Scotland. On his knees Count Benedict had besought him to hire Henry the Angevin, the famous knight-at-arms who had won renown with the Swan of Bohun and the White Lion of March. Twice daily the Duke now stripped, allowing himself to be oiled and pummelled, testing himself against Black Fulk, Dietrich, Edward of the Four, charging at the pole, swaying with axe and lance, carrying off the poised gage at his spear's point.

All the Court was livening. Authorities on tournaments were being carefully studied: Philip the Fair, John of Anjou, James the Deathless. Master Brede was busy designing costumes: young girls' hair was being worn shorter, in compliment to the fighter's art, and dress would be severer. Bloodshed was to come. As he thought of it the colour mounted in Count Benedict's withered cheeks, his bearing stiffened, his mind trundled with formalities and his long yellow hand curled round a lance long dropped and foresworn.

TEN

In the last week of April the Duchess Katherine sought morning audience of the Duke. Only in stress or emergency did this occur, this departure from order, and some grumbling was aroused by the necessity to alter the times.

The Duke, attended by his page René, was in a white throne-room. He rose to greet her as she entered, the Lady Joanna behind her.

She made her reverence, then stood, caped in old-gold and blue, a few red blossoms amid the jewels on her head-piece, a Ring of Peace on her finger.

'My loving Lord, my heart is filled with gratitude at your receiving me on so splendid and lustred a morning.'

He smiled, carefully watching her. 'To hasten to my Lady's summons is to dance at the bell of Paradise, and to grant her requests is to have opened the burnished gate, instead of wandering where foolish feet lead.'

She hesitated, glanced first at René's fair polished face between its long, brown widths of hair, then at Joanna. Neither could move, for the Duke, acknowledging her desire only by silence, remained waiting, alert, even hopeful for a sign of weakness, and finally she was forced to speak outright.

'My Lord, has the Lady Joanna your permission to withdraw?'

The Duke seated himself on the narrow, glistening throne. There was no other chair or stool so she had to remain standing. He smiled again. 'Though the beauty and graciousness of the Lady Joanna carry but the

74

reflection of her mistress' favouring lights, we cannot but hope that she will remain here with us to give us the gladness of enjoying the purity of her gracious smile.'

'My Lord.' Her eyes implored him. That such an audience should not be private was unprecedented, almost sinful. René was pale, Joanna troubled.

Disregarding his wife's agitation, Simon turned aside, taunting beneath his deliberation. 'Lady Joanna, while Her Grace composes the words for which she has been received, allow us to compliment you further. Time has no fangs in your admired features, madame, nor soils the brightness of your flowing hair. Tell us when your next birthday falls, and Her Grace and I can make our token, and set an amend for Time's small triumph.'

He laughed politely, then, covering her confusion, continued. 'And yet, the only true birthday is when by merit we increase our souls.' He nodded at Katherine, made as if to relent, perhaps may even have wished to relent, then instead, resumed, playing upon her dejection. 'How many birthdays, then, have you and I achieved together, Your Grace? Our nuptial night,' he said with meaning, 'was that a birthday? For did we not gain lasting grace and unity? And the gift of our sweet Lord Charles, hairy as a Poitevin and twice as loud? So handsome and without guile, the prince of pure delight! Or,' he added maliciously, for he knew why she had come, 'our first Hunt? Her Grace,' he looked towards René who, knowing his master, was now almost shivering, 'wept at the tall stag's death. She spoilt the bright day with her tender heart and her fine soul, and my people declared that I was a robber, having stolen a saint from God's palace!'

'My Lord.' She whispered it, but her eyes had steadied above her flushed cheek. Aware of this, he sat up brusquely, mirthlessly, considered, then, with an affected laugh, signed to the boy.

'My good René, here we have three fully-fledged voices and your own delicate range. Her Grace has a loving heart and welcomes a well-versed canzone: and our Lady Joanna sings from out of heaven itself: and you and I, my friend, sing well enough as sons of Red Adam should, though we are no lovers. Or do I mistake you? But run for your lute, my fine fellow, and lend us a note, and the four of us shall sing of heavenly love and earthly desire and so pass the hour. Thanks be to Her Grace for providing us with so joyous a morning.'

The three waited for the page to return, the Lady Joanna not daring to raise her eyes. Must such a song indeed be sung its sense would be blasphemous, and its tender sound from the devil. They waited, held by the lure of some strange decay.

'Will Her Grace be hunting?'

A meaning look flitted between two ladies. It had been rumoured earlier that the Duchess had particularly desired to ride in the May Day Hunt. Others asserted that she had commanded a scarlet and green skirt for the occasion.

The Court had risen early on May Day, the first of Joymonth. A few ladies had kissed the dew to revive their beauty. The Duke himself in golden boots winged at the heel, had climbed the Arch Tower to face the rising sun, and shoot twelve arrows at the four quarters, while an immense crowd below, citizens, travellers, courtiers, peasants all mingled together and applauded, trained on the solitary figure above, his face and bow raised to the flame in the sky.

For two hours the archers had been shooting at the sun. The hawthorn had been plucked. Already the dancers were circling about Thor's Yard, a heavy green and red maypole in the fishmarket where even the empalsied old men were cackling and raising skinny hands to the sun.

Would the Duchess be hunting? Gossip drew breath, then hastened on. Slowly the wide Marshal's Hall filled. Noblemen sauntered in complicated files with retinues of pages in silver and green. Slender young men, their blue garters set with samite and pearl, stood by the walls, hawks hooded and motionless on their wrists. Ladies were holding small grey Camargue ponies. Green huntsmen between the groups uttered sharp archaic cries. Above them rose the Palace Walls encrusted with stone cords of grapes and leaves, carved giants grasping shields and crossing swords, impish leering faces half-hidden by foliage, lean satyr-feet.

In an instant all became inattentive, pretending to notice nothing. The gay, easy scene stiffened and dried on the air. The Duchess had been observed on a balcony, with her tire-women, gazing outwards above the throng, to the chequer-board of gardens where already the roses were budding, the Hermes and Bacchus and Phoebus gleaming through young leaf, the child sky reflected in

77

roseate pools, the peacocks merging into the new blossom of the Duke's walk. But there were no other eyes for leaves, for peacocks, for valerian. Already it was realised that Katherine would remain in the Palace, ignored by the Duke, and that for her there was no May.

The crowd thickened. Several unfamiliar faces were about. The Bastard of Lorraine, who had started the fashion for slashed hose: the Bishop of Vaux, with an uncanny tale of the loyal and discerning Richard of Gloucester: a cousin of the Visconti sheathed in lilac-silk with long trailing sleeves, and telling of Chardelory of Turin who condemned men to imprisonment half-way up a sheer cliff, a foot from hell, waiting for them to go mad and hurl themselves down.

At the gates under the hawks, the beggars, alert for largesse, were whispering that the Duke had ordered the sun to shine.

Trumpets sounded twice. Cavalcades parted for the gliding bodies, the sinuous, minutely swaying heads, the jewelled eyes of the leopards, led on scarlet chains. A long company of squires followed, each leading his lord's horse, many of which were snuffling uneasily, warned by the leopards. Already beyond the gates were three outriders in blue, green and white and encased in their winding hunting-horns.

In all the horses' tails fresh leaves had been tied. From the hooded gerfalcons, unmoving on wrists, sounded the tiny jingle of almost invisible bells. The hunters were carefully arranging themselves in fitting order, the Grand Huntsman and prelates taking precedence. Then the trumpets rang again, three times, for the Duke, small horns announcing the readiness of the ladies. Caps were removed, plumes swept the smooth lemon-coloured stone as the Duke emerged from under a canopy, smiling, preparing to receive his horse. He was in green with white and blood-red sleeves, golden coronet and spurs, cornelian belt, an arm-band of leaves. His hand rested on the shoulder of the Noble Friend, Viscount Charles at his back, likewise with leaves on his arm and in his blue pointed cap.

The Duke smiled again and quoted so that others could hear:

> 'Satyrs are awake,
>   Dancing the Dryads,'

turning for the Chevalier to conclude:

>   'The nymphs in the brake
>   Kindling for his sake,
>   Lit with new fires.'

More trumpets, then horns, the notes climbing in irregular groups of four. The Duke swung himself up. Charles and Young Roger did likewise. Father and son were still not yet on terms. As if mocking, the Duke was retaining that portrait, and the boy's anger could not be restrained.

All were now horsed. Horns re-echoed, sounding the overture call. Slowly the tall intricate gates opened, the beggars squawled and clutched; from a portcullised archway hounds trotted forward, running to heel once the leopards had passed. But still the Duchess and her women remained on their balcony, at this distance motionless, as if painted, no-one daring to incline towards her after the Duke's deliberate rebuff. Soon Flavius would be creeping forward to jeer at her.

The main array, silvery and jostling, the Duke at its head, the Huntsman, Viscount and Ladies immediately behind, moved slowly through the streets, through Saint James' Gate to the meadows a-slope the river, grass and leaves green as hope, water gleaming like handfuls of crushed florins. A cuckoo was heard from the Mother Spinney. All, the Chevalier whispered to Lady Anna his titular mistress, was the equivalent of music, the horns and trumpets only confirming what already was.

A small trumpet cried that a heron had been sighted. At a sign from the Duke the ladies cantered forward, dropping reins and drawing out small bows from saddle-bags. A moment later, to delight, the heron was falling and a dog rushing to catch it as it reached the ground.

The morning seemed to turn and wind effortlessly, its speed caught from the gliding movement of the Hunt, displaying, through glistening pockets of air, bunches of hawthorn, the dew scarcely dead on the blossom: also peasants kneeling about a Robin and Marion, and a dead man lying by the roadside, three fingers outstretched behind his head to show that he was a perjurer. Once, between slotted boughs as the hawk rose and the whistle shrilled, the lords and ladies saw in a quiver of Time a Wild Man, leafed, with marigolds in his cap. They ranged on, past high stones erected by peoples who had once lived here but who had long since been driven to hills and marshes, had grown smaller and smaller and, for the most part, had long vanished altogether, but for moments of trickery. Once the leopards were released, to maul a

standing ox, though for this no horns deigned to call.
And the morning expanded, clawing at the softening
horizons, seeking new colours, new freedoms. Trumpets
sang in slow extended chorus, one seizing and enlarging
upon the others, the notes full and melodious in the
endless air: they could be felt climbing, solid and
glinting, floating over forest and hill and the broad
coloured range of the Duchy.

The hunters set spurs down a pearled waving sweep
of meadowed down, leaving behind the leopards, that
were now led off down the royal road to be admired and
feasted in the small town ahead. At the bottom, set close
to the green thickets, silently waited a vast satin tent
embossed with the gilt mottoes and red arms of the
House. Long tables were piled with goblets, bottles,
caskets of walnuts, olives, capers, quinces, meaty Florentines, slices of pork, quail and fowl on skewers. The
hounds were collected under the trees, snuffling and
rooting amongst heavy twisted roots.

All dismounted, repairing to the tent. The Duke stood
drinking a little apart, his eyes behind their indolence
missing nothing. Two ladies were whispering to the
Visconti, who raked them with narrow adroit glances.
Viscount Charles, flushed and sinewy, had gripped Young
Roger and was kissing him in sudden frenzy. He said in
his breathless way, 'He only pretended to die,' adding in
a lower, more urgent tone, 'I wanted to love him,' and
stared in sudden dismay at Roger, who nodded, feigning
to understand.

One of the court poets, in green silks, who had ridden
beforehand with the retainers, was already reciting lines

from his Ballade that he had been composing throughout:

> 'At the green and dewy hour
> Duke Simon rides a-pace.'

Punctiliously, but assuming a slight weariness, the Duke addressed his companion. 'In what does the merit of hunting consist, my lord?' As though he had already rehearsed the words.

'Day and Night are the same, Heraclitus said. But the Hunt breaks the circle, leaps from the dross.' Uncertain of the Duke's mood, the Chevalier gave a gentle appeasing smile.

The sun had attained full height above the trees. The tops glistened. Powerful heat steamed from the dry undergrowth where celandines wavered in pointed, delicate frettery. Horns sounded the Second Stage, the ladies doffed and gathered in a square to wave farewell. At a signal the outriders galloped away through the trees: the hounds, freed by berners, set up a deep prolonged bay, then, with a flourish, the Duke mounted, spurred off, oblivious to all, setting the pace. The rest, after three calls, plunged after him, the Viscount in the lead.

Riding was swift, under branch, under leaf. A horn cried in top note for a boar, then was echoed from far away to the right, and reinforced ahead by a sequence, 'The Queen of England's Slipper'. The Duke swerved outwards towards a clearing, outmatching all but the hardest, though the Chevalier still maintained himself almost at his side, his thoughts tangled with speed and green and queer recollections of the Red King of the English. In these swerves, in this speed, this elation of dust, sunlight, panting vicious dogs, and the victim ahead . . . was it a boar, was it a stag with forefoot destined for the Duke . . . ? lurked music and the dance. Difficult was it to determine where riding ended and music began. Speed of horses was reflected in the body: blood rushed and the heart soared: songs abounded, unheard but sharp and penetrating as flame. Did the stag exist, was it there, crashing ahead: or did it live merely in these intent transfixed faces, this singing blood? Were they hunting, or was it they who were mysteriously in flight? Here, the fleeting moment was like a certain turn in a battle when, for a dazzling space, you cannot decide whether you are in victory or rout, poised in a bloody and instinctive commingling of both. Pace and mindlessness, landscape of unicorn, bright air above the moon.

Horns were soon calling to each other from all parts of the forest, and within an hour the hounds had already killed and a fanfare had sounded over a gory, quivering boar, now to be cut and unlaced. But the Duke, a slight sarcasm at his lips, was ahead again, his horse flecked and damp. Now he was alone, the Chevalier beaten at last, outridden, discarded, and even the wilder courtiers warily keeping due pace from their master. He had emerged from the trees and was riding up hills above a valley, meeting the sky, an entire landscape of river and castle, hamlet and barn moving below. But another rider darted from the forest, pursuing: the Viscount, spurring, stuttering with passion to overtake. Now the Hour of Diana was fading into that of Mars, and the new and rival planet infected the two rivals riding between.

The Duke smiled shortly and raced forward, dust

clouding the path. Ever higher, into the sky, the air hard and gripping, shadows leaping, always a little ahead, and perhaps a stag belling far-off. His spurs dug into the sodden mass with the mad sensations of forcing a woman. Behind lay the boar, tusked and wicked, garlanded, giant in death, bedded and mantled in fiery blood. Oh the instant as the beast faltered, stopping sheer, and turned, tusks shining, bristles rising, eyes tiny and red: the shout as the hounds pounced and the lance was raised; then charging home, ramming itself through skin and vein and bone, blood spurting like ancient treasure, so that your body longed to be stripped and hurled forward tense and naked and, with horns, trumpets, cymbals marshalled, to be bathed and renewed in hot steaming mass.

In ambushed, heart-flung desperation the Duke pulled up. Only a few feet away, falling many hundred feet, was the cliff, waiting to trap and pull him over, to shatter him on the rocks, from this height so small that they seemed left over from play, but which would, within a breath, tower over his smashed frame and call to the black crows lurking in the sky. Forgetting the riders behind, two now as Young Roger was following his master with face white and strained, eyes unyielding, the Duke patted his gasping horse and continued to gaze down. The cliff awaited him with its devilish and sickening temptations. A hydra-head was lurking below: a dim eye peered from the depths: ultimately a watcher would become those depths, without soul or grace yet, in an evil way, satisfied.

Viscount Charles was pounding up. The father's remote, oddly fragile figure could not halt his impetuosity. He charged towards the unmarked cliff edge. Nor did the Duke make any warning sign, and it was the boy's horse that of itself pulled up short, alongside the Duke, snorting with fear, appalled by the swaying chaos at its feet.

Charles blanched, his eyes were left stark and isolated: only Young Roger from behind saved him from toppling. The Duke remained very still, becoming stronger now as his son faded. Then, leaning forwards as if his words could physically injure the older man, his weapon-hand shaking, the Viscount gasped:

'My painting. You devils, you all want to cheat me. To rob me.' His eyes recovered, widened and he seemed only now to recognise the yearning, tortured chasm above which they were drawn. Roger had to hold him even further, feeling him lurch and tremble as he muttered, 'You wanted me to fall. You wanted me in hell.'

The Duke regarded him. Beneath dark-brown fringe and coronet his face was quiet, persuasive, at ease. Between golden clumps, both the ominous, quivering blotch and Charles' eyes seemed to be eating into his flesh, tainting the body so transfixed with feeling. But the Duke said nothing, the sarcasm was back on his lips and, baffled, his son choked, then pulled savagely at his horse, lashing it, speeding away, furious, on and on, not seeing Roger flung off by his sudden turn and lying prone and bleeding, until the Duke awoke and rode up and disdainfully bent over him with quick skilled fingers.

ELEVEN

THE Court was ranged in the Knights' Hall according to
due order under the tapestries of the Joust of Touraine.
It was the celebration of the Duke's marriage-day, on
which many dues had to be paid.

To the fore stood Knights of the Fleece, armoured,
carrying golden helmets. To their left were the scarlet
Cardinal-Legate, the Archbishop robed and mitred,
together with the Ambassador from the Podesta. On a
small throne facing them sat Duchess Katherine, in water-
blue to display her love of Divine Works. On the wall
behind, a black velvet curtain had been hung.

The Duke, who had been standing beside Katherine,
now advanced, hand in hand with his Heir. Father
and son were armoured in hard grey, and bareheaded:
brown against gold. Squires held their purple-plumed
casques.

'We welcome you, lords and vassals. It is our privilege.'

Many noblemen were in red, strewn with bells, trinkets,
thin jangling strips of silver. They stood behind the
statuesque knights, who had already paid their reverence.
The ladies were with them, in long chequered gowns and
diamond-buckled feet.

At a fanfare all but the knights knelt, sweeping their
large coiled caps and, in leek-green, the Five Lords of the
Marches advanced bearing on silvered trays handfuls of
roses, to be presented on bended knees as tribute for their
estates. There succeeded two lords in flat caps, delegates
from the University Chapter presenting a painted manu-

script displaying a Spartan hero betrayed to the magistrates by a kiss.

Finally, led by the Knights of the Fleece, the massed company came forward, then, one by one, kissed the Duke's hand, bowed low to the Duchess, then hastened to congratulate the Viscount, over whose shoulders had now been placed a robe of May-green to show his love and hopes of Isabel, his betrothed.

Where was she now, it was wondered: under duress with false Rainault: on her way to seek the Duke's protection, riding to the Tournament? For some months there had been no word of her. Rumours had been speeding that morning from one bright face to another of the new and ferocious insult to the Duke said to have been uttered by the Prince of Utrecht. 'My lord Raymond had it from his sister. She has heard about Rainault, that hog, that Templar . . . I would not give a brawn pudding for his love.'

The Duke had stood for several hours receiving roses, jewels, standards. Behind him, his tiny bells quivering, and supreme in a jasmine-yellow costume, moved Flavius the Nose, who now whispered: 'You are the wind. You ride where you listeth and you will never stay. The wind can bring tears to a man's eyes: it can strip him and smart him. Yet it is a thing of naught. A child can make it and the Devil raise it.'

When all had been completed according to custom the Duke spoke:

'Dearly Loved and Trustworthy . . .' before turning back to that black velvet curtain, straight and solemn and mysterious. Throughout it had been there, attracting

all eyes, concealing its wonder. At a sign from Count
Benedict, two pages pulled away the curtain, and with
an elaborate bow the Duke spoke again.

'My Lords . . . I present to you and my dear son, the
Lady Isabel. Serve her well, and God in His Concern will
reward you now and Hereafter.'

Exclamations flew at once, admiring and dreamy. The
dark eyes of Lady Isabel filled the Hall, flowing out of the
oval face: that celebrated face, pale and hard as a bone,
only the small mouth broken by an indecisive smile.

Congratulations now swarmed over the young Viscount who received them with a heavy sulkiness mingled
with awkwardness. The knights drew swords in unison,
struck sparks from the stone and shouted, 'Long life to
our Sovereign Liege and his children Charles and Isabel:
Isabel and Charles! May the Duke and his Duchess live
for ever. Isabel and Charles!'

Katherine sat very still on her throne, acknowledging
nothing, because of her position. Her tall head-piece concealed her hair entirely, and, in contrast to Isabel, her
face was soft and as if unseeing, or seeing only into herself.
But perhaps for the first time men noticed faint lines
beneath her eyes, a slight darkening of her skin. Whatever
her thoughts, however, she maintained herself like a
bastion. She was Duchess.

The Cardinal-Legate uttered felicitations in Latin.
Before he had concluded he was roughly poked in the
back by Flavius:

'From a robin's nest take eggs,
And you'll break your legs.'

88

The afternoon was passed out of doors in the sunlight. The walk to Mars Field was pleasant, the Fountain had been completed, and many were hastening to see whether the effigy of the Lady bore features to resemble Isabel, whose apartments were rising so rapidly. The Unicorn was there, gentle and gleaming, laying his head on her lap, but the lady's features had not yet been modelled.

Talk of Rainault was everywhere heard, and applause was given when Master Egyptian pronounced that He of Utrecht had been born under an evil star. Unfortunately, three different horoscopes had already been delivered, foretelling that he would die of Plague, would vanish in the East, would survive a fiery ordeal.

On the city walls pictures had been scratched of Rainault obscenely maimed, and of the Ram pike-stricken in heart and genitals. In the Palace too the painters were busy caricaturing him, and Master Eck, lately arrived from Leyden, attracted much laughter by giving him a curved, immense nose.

'He's a Jew. A positive Turk. A money-bags. But the Duke will save us.'

'But look over here. What is this? I see a lame leg! I see a spurious arm!'

'There are eyes that can tell,' the Count of the Forests said in his slow way, 'that the high and most excellent great porker Rainault will beget no more bastards.'

Neglecting no opportunity, Count Benedict had also set the poets to mock him, gibing at him for having exhausted his manhood.

'An empty sack . . .
        The Lord Rainault,'
in an effort to make this indeed so.

All the while the chroniclers were writing away dili-
gently in shadowy alcoves. 'And it was at this time that
the said Rainault began to make ready his preparations
for the most famed of all passages-at-arms, beginning
his journey with the most devout prayers and ministra-
tions, according to his wont. But such travail was as
naught in comparison with that of his adversary, the
most pious and high-born Duke.'

In the Spring Pavilion, built for a former Duchess to
observe showers and sunlight, set above the gentle blur
of the herb gardens, a Council was sitting. The Duke was
not present. The lords had bowed to his chair and poured
wine over the stones. Grouped around the heavy table
were the Archbishop, Count Benedict, the Lord Estrienne; the Count of the March, here for the Duke's Day
and maintaining his prerogative: the Almoner and the
Huntsman. At a side-table, bent deferentially over his
parchments, sat Jew Plate.

The Archbishop said reasonably, with some apology,
'I would ask you to remember, under God, that tourna-
ments were condemned and gainsaid by our Father
Innocent at the Lateran Council.'

The Count of the March, sturdy, swarthy, swallowed
wine more noisily than was seemly. 'Without the rigours
of field and tourney the common weal grows rank and
we ourselves overblown and dull.'

Count Benedict nodded assent. The Archbishop

glanced smilingly at them all. He enjoyed such discussions. But a fine ridge of irritation spoilt his white forehead as he saw that the Lord Estrienne was thinking of something else. He said carefully:

'Holy Church accepts this in her wisdom. Was there not war even in heaven? It is not the battlefield we condemn, for conflict, the philosopher tells us, is the father of all. Nay, rather the pride that engenders it. And primarily the swollen spiritual pride that victory and defeat alike bestow upon lords.'

Count Benedict shook his head. 'Pride separates us from the beasts, maintains us in fine measure, Your Grace. Pride in our vigour keeps us upright: upright in our bodies, upright in our souls. Pride reveals itself in the beauty of young manhood. The field and tourney keep man at his fullest pitch, like a bow admirably strung and drawn by a fighter of ability. He becomes a banner stiff in the breeze, the high track of an eagle, the mountain's peak. Who can conclude the effect of man's soul by his seeing his lord's standard unfurled?'

The Huntsman intervened. 'Is it true, Your Grace, that under certain circumstances the Church admits that Ethiopians, Moors, Parthians have white souls?'

'The Church has many secrets,' the Archbishop crossed his hands in slow, replete satisfaction, 'secrets which she does not reveal except to the initiate. We would not wilfully demoralise our children. Confronted by truths too great to bear, the mind goes mad and sins.'

At 'initiate' the Lord Estrienne made a dry, secretive grimace. He looked up. 'Let us regard facts. Facts stripped of the devious, the specious and the disgusting, have no need to be concealed except for interested purposes. A certain Agnes was canonised for not washing. And if you look at your Lord's standard for long enough you can make it fall down. Let us remember that ideas, however divine, however courtly, however knightly, are the fruit of physical experience. That man is made in God's image has a further interpretative possibility that cannot escape even His Grace, though he will never concern himself to make it public. What we are dealing with is not the nature of combats and tournaments, for that is self-evident, nor the virtues of pride, for what is pride but the fullness of nature unimpeded? Nor with man's need for the Church, for who am I to die for heresy? We are discussing the position of the Countess Isabel and her virtues several and manifold.'

'And these are . . . ?'

The Lord Estrienne picked them off on his fingers. 'The rights over seven hundred fishponds. The revenues of the County of Mayence. The stewardships of Hey, Kerina, Vallade and Havet. The river-mouth of La Pont. The five windmills of Suçar. Rights over the commons of Largent, Verence, Clemence and Yvres. The island of Menier. Hunting rights in the forests of Vance and ninefold-dues in the diocese of Saint Sigismund. Seventy and ten hundreds in silver. The castle of Hill-Prépé. Alternate rights to the Fealty of Brabant. The Wardship of Pontieu. The succession to the Banneret of Stret. The titular lordship and quarterings of Clare. The Cadetship of the Barony of Lavoisir. The Reversion Chancellorship to the University of Tuckor.'

Grey steep heads nodded. The atmosphere, formerly

vague and luxuriant, in tune with the drowsy imper-
manent butterflies, sleek leaves, the gracious patina of
sunlight, rue, shadowy mint, borage, water, dwindled to
the fixed and immediate and the Count of the March
gulped loudly, then laughed.

'Such powers! Such grand effects! No wonder our
Rainault wants to learn his lesson, to shed his energies.
No wonder he seeks his troves, eh!'

Count Benedict half-rose, but the Lord Estrienne
forestalled him. 'But will he come?' he demanded, his
irony so pronounced that all faces turned at him, heavy
with reproach.

TWELVE

To-day there was no Council. The Duke lay alone on his couch listening to his pages in the adjoining room. He had dreamed, or thought he had dreamed, of moving stones by song to form a city.

He was lying in the Forest Room. Under an arras two hounds drowsed, their flews dripping on the shepherdess, birds, river enscrolled on the carpet. The arras, all peregrine and cobalt, showed Alexander dying at Babel. On the small domed ceiling, gold birds hung against a dawn sky.

The Room was termed Forest because of the picture immediately opposite the Duke's eye. This had been drawn in lost Tartar inks. In the early morning you saw a wood, dark leaves arrested like frozen tears and, beneath a tall wood-cutter, a girl with a doll and tiny birds on a branch above a pool. Later, as the light turned, the wood became blurred and swollen, only the wood-cutter remaining distinct, the girl and birds vanished. Young and strong he stood entire, with axe gleaming. By afternoon, however, he had aged and shrunk, new inks were exposed, making the pool a rushing river, the birds one bird shrill and unappeasable. The child had returned, kneeling in fear, and the doll was lost. The forest deepened in the hush. By evening, in dangerous twilight there were only huge separate shadows but, as the torches were lit, the whole reappeared: the woodsman was standing in calm, secure light, with the girl, the doll, the birds, the distinct protecting trees.

The Duke had once remarked that it was here in this small painted room that it was possible to move the hearts of ancestors. The Forest, notwithstanding, was silent, though in the East such pictures had been known to speak.

Pages' voices drifted to him through the violet, curtained arch.

'There's loving in Paradise.'

'How do you know it?'

'I wager there is. Playing odds and evens with Her whom you know.'

'There must be wine too.'

'I'll exchange loving for wining.'

'An exchange. But you are too young to know pleasures.'

'No. I can love and drink.'

Behind them was the sound of masons preparing the apartments for Countess Isabel. Immediately beneath the window were the movements of children.

The Duke roused himself and, knowing that he was unobserved, quietly removed the lattice. The children were playing seekers. A thin file moved in and out of the shadows, their rings snatching at the sunlight. A remark of the Lord Estrienne's came to him as he watched the swaying, almost soundless line.

'To charm the Snake is also to control yourself. Control life and you overcome Nature. Overcome Nature and you can create God.'

Youth still remained in the Duke's face, but it almost vanished as his brows met. That the Snake, guardian of riches, could assume diverse shapes yet remain One, that it renewed its skin in season, moved without limbs, could meet its own tail . . . these facts had endless meanings and frequently the Duke had the sensation that his former tutor did not see with his eyes alone, but that there were appearances and motives that even Dukes did not penetrate without help from tutors.

The children below continued their game. The Duke watched. The dance of life was a circle, a straight line. Then suddenly they disappeared and the courtyard stood dry and empty in meshed, yellow lights.

The Duke stood as near irresolute as he ever permitted himself to be. The sunlit day would be long and he had much to accomplish. Already he had broken fast, on a heron's leg that had lain in the earth a week: he had greeted the Duchess: listened for a moment to Flavius babbling of Amloti, the Fool of Denmark, whose uncle slew his brother in the green wood. This had led to considerations of the ogre who treads on you in sleep. But Flavius was tedious on a warm morning and could be dismissed to preach to the peacocks, or sit with squires inventing unpleasant stories about the Lord Estrienne. That Lord paid no court to Flavius and was therefore much abused by him. The Architect General had then presented plans for an oak and ivory Pavilion, a Tapestry Workshop, and a Workers' House in the Royal Clothieries.

He struck a gong. The pages hurried in, sinking to one knee. The Duke held up his left hand. At once Pierre vanished, then returned with a goblet. His master drank thoughtfully. The wine was chill, as though a ghost had breathed on it.

Now the day must be allowed to proceed. It was as though it had been noosed and chained: now the noose was unlinked and Time slid gently away, towards whither? At once the Chaplain was announced, a meagre yellowish old man with merry eyes and erratic disposition. As the Duke's confessor he was allowed to be seated.

The two men nodded familiarly and the Chaplain was soon mentioning Pelagius the Damned, who had denied the heritage of Adam's sin to man. The Duke merely sighed and, shifting the talk, the Chaplain, Van Meeg, quoted hopefully, 'He who wishes to convince himself of the presence of devils has but to surround his bed with sifted cinders and the next morning he will see the imprint of a cock's foot.'

They both laughed gently, then the Duke shrugged. To a pupil of the Lord Estrienne it was not that there were no devils: they had names and therefore proved themselves. They were not, nevertheless, what were generally supposed, and the difficulty was in finding anything to say, either about them or to them.

The Duke and Van Meeg exchanged some conventional chatter about the belief, probably erroneous but not damnable, that the True Cross had been grown from seeds planted by Seth in the mouth of the Lord Adam. It was not a confessional morning, which relieved both men.

The Chaplain was succeeded by a college of Doctors for the monthly scrutiny of the Duke's blood, for if dukes decay the land rots. Again the Duke sighed. He was never ill, for a long time the apothecaries had been in despair: His Grace's self-control mocked their calling. Only last week a new recipe had arrived: moss from skulls of the hanged to relieve fits. Unfortunately the Duke never had fits and the moss had to be wasted in the public hospitals and the monasteries.

After the Doctors the Duke received his son. The Viscount had been reported by his tutors as having drawn many figures, half-human and half-animal on floors; but Duke Simon disregarded this.

'Well, my son . . .'

The word 'son' annoyed him. He did not feel so old. Indeed, with bruised features, sulky expression, his burnished hair at this moment rather dirty, Charles himself surely 'seemed' the elder. They stood facing each other.

'I shall ride,' the boy said grudgingly, 'I shall ride with Roger.' Looking at his feet he said again, 'I shall ride.'

Since May Day neither had mentioned the approaching marriage. It lay between them like music waiting to be sounded, like a hawk to be tamed, like a text to be examined, like a space to be filled. But this morning it seemed unreal, too distant, an island seen across waters, and you look again and it is not there and perhaps never was.

Left alone, the Duke recognised that he was standing very still, though the sun had not yet entered the House of Noon. A parchment demanded him from the table, a complaint to pass on to the Lord Mayor that the barbers were neglecting their charge of driving lepers from the city gates. He ignored it, having promised to receive the Chevalier Stephen, who had dreamed last Sunday of ice and horses and had fashioned a poem thereby.

They continued the theme started at last night's supper.

'Because poetry, my dearest Lord, expresses in mortal and sensual terms what the priest expresses in religious and the alchemist in scientific terms. Our new art is not a means to piety nor a lesson in devotion, nor the decoration to a prayer, but it brings the old backgrounds into full view, to be contemplated for their own truths.'

'The Thing in Itself, as our Paymaster General would say. The Thing in Itself. We are all his pupils and in the worthiest of all fiefs. Should we not then think of heaven itself as those uncharted shoals of the mind which, by despatching dreams and ghosts, gives us our noblest preliminaries to art?'

'Then the common people are nearer heaven than we are, for you and I, my Lord, have left so little of our minds to explore.'

The Chevalier giggled unexpectedly, then, noticing the Duke's sombre gaze, said, 'If we could but go back. Back. Further than old Benedict's knights and ladies. Much further. As it is, the world ages. There can be few years left. I dreamed once that we can be rescued only by he who neither sees nor walks, and who hears without ears.'

'Sing to me, my Lord.' The Duke gazed at the tall unsteady nobleman, and a page hurried forward with a lute. The tiny notes pricked the warm hushed forenoon.

'For Love, the singer cries
And the blossom quivers,
Without Love the heart dies,
And the violet withers.'

The Chevalier was singing, but the Duke again sighed. He must soon visit the armouries to prepare for his bout with Angevin Henry under the stern eye of Count Benedict.

This done, he drank wine, refreshed himself, dismissed his attendants and moved alone into the gardens under shadowy, rustling cedars and chestnuts. All was hushed save for the hurrying of birds and from the far corner of the Palace where, in some gallery, a motet was being rehearsed, directed by the Architect General, whose profession had made him expert in all manner of music. The undercurrent of virginals suited the blobs and dabs of colour, here in the gardens where the peacocks moved on their lawns and a golden pheasant stood momentarily molten in sunlight, and pigeons settled at various heights in the bosquets. Here where he stood, bees were penetrating columbine and penny-royal: the sunlight lay flat and taut on a wide square of sage: early poppies showed fires and, by the low reddening wall, rose myrtle, pomegranate, oleander.

The Duke sauntered further, past a thick constellation of lilies where, as if in echo, the swans floated and dipped on their coppery lake beneath walnut foliage, and the egrets moved in and out of bulrushes.

He saw that he was no longer alone. A young girl of the Court was standing by the Nereid Fountain as if reading it. A bell sounded from an invisible tower.

Appropriately, he realised that the Hour of Venus had begun. He walked on and, startled, she turned and immediately gave the wide extended curtsey.

Gravely he raised her up, recognising the pink moulded face under the velvet head-dress in which lay a tiny emerald lance, in honour of the coming Tournament. 'Your Grace!' she murmured, colouring. They stood together, contemplating the green slender nereid, sadly crouching to watch herself in the water. Half-forgotten stories hung about her. A girl had loved the moon and drowned herself. Another had turned to fire, to water, to escape yet finally enslave the knight who pursued her. A harp had sung at a feast, accusing the bright-eyed lord who sat at the king's right hand, though his own hand was tainted.

'*He brought her a basin of marble stone to catch her life-blood in.*'

The Duke looked away. The lassitude that had threatened him briefly retreated. His voice was very quiet. 'Do you love me?'

She hesitated. By convention, only truth should be uttered to the Duke. Hurriedly he moved aside, then, with formality, allowing her no time to speak further, he drew his silver dagger and cut off several blooms, choosing harsh reds and yellows though his face now expressed nothing. Understanding their message, she accepted them with humility, knowing that she had missed a trick in the play, perhaps the play itself.

'My Lord, I revere you as my Duke and Liege. I tread in your footsteps. Whatever I can give is your due . . .'

But, already disappointed, he had left her, withdrawing

into the thickening haze of thyme, heliotrope and pear-tree: rose-bud and daphne, the missal-world of which he was more verily supreme. Drawn by his obsessions he approached the Five Gardens of Love, each with its intricate mottoes and analogies patterned from stone and bush and blossom. The box hedges in all their convolutions and mazes in the Garden of Tragic Love: the soft blues and pinks overlapping in the Garden of Tender Love: the hard green spikes and thorns crossing in the Garden of Violent Love: the tumescent roses, balanced lilies, misty lavender in the Garden of Married Love: the convulsed blacks and crimsons, the blood-reds and agonised purples in the Garden of Mad Love. And the sundials, and beasts, and warning or taunting gods.

Almost at once he was disturbed. A new bell was sounding. The motet had long finished and sunlight was thrusting more sharply through the branches.

In the Disrobing Room the chess-men were reflected in various mirrors, echoed above and below him, their midget battle alive with possibilities: with feints and raids and ambushes, though it must always remain locked within itself, unable to conceive adventure or crusade.

He stared at them as if rebuking them for what they were not, then stepped away as abruptly as he had left the lady who must still be by the fountain, bemoaning her lost opportunity. Then he seated himself before the largest mirror, shifting it so as to empty its surface of the silent, poised chess-men. Momentarily he held it. En-scrolled at the edges with a rout of satyrs and angels, it had been receiving him since his childhood: it was his confidant, his most ancient tutor, ultimately his blood-brother. Yet it was insufficient. He laid it against his cheek, then replaced it on its ledge, continuing to gaze into it as if expecting a face to appear behind his shoulder.

He was singing to himself, wordlessly, and the squires hovering outside crept away, avoiding each other's eyes. Finally he desisted, said aloud, 'Isabel', gazing into himself, waiting to be interrupted, already ill-humoured.

THIRTEEN

'THERE was Earl Manfred who dreamed one night of a fair and high-born lady, and he sold his manors and with a solitary squire set out into the world to find her. Occasionally we heard news of him, rumours of him. From amongst the mountains of the Assassins, from the Spanish kingdoms, from the city of the Emperor of the Greeks. But he never came back.'

Count Benedict repeated with satisfaction, and pride, 'He never came back. It was many years ago. He will not return.'

The gaily-clad lordlings exchanged glances. Various people at Court would remind each other with shrugs and affectation that the old man was comically antique. He still maintained the ceremony of the Cou: whenever a child was born in his household the father had to pretend to be bearing it, to ward off devils from the mother. Furthermore, there was his absurd map of a land that no longer existed and, according to Master Remy, had never existed, though the Count had pored over it for so many hours.

He had been speaking of warriors long dead: Montfort and Manny, Chandos, du Guesclin, Edward of Aquitaine, Edward of Carnarvon, Richard the Jongleur, Conrad of the Mount, and those earlier knights who could ride and touch hands with Sir Hector and Sir Bors, Lancelot the Light Bringer and Tristan of the Spear, Achilles and Hannibal, the Lord Eneas and his weeping, foresworn Dido. Of knights who bound one hand behind them in the fight: who fought naked: who threw away their shield for their lady's kirtle: knights standing all night with bowed heads on the field after victory: knights who heard seals singing off the holy rocks of Ireland: knights from Normandy, all in iron, their stirrups enabling them to bear heavy armour and wield axe and lance against Saracen and Saxon, Italian and Algerian. Knights of the Star who, bound by oath, refused to leave stricken Agincourt and preferred in honour to be slaughtered by the English King.

Several glances of incomprehension passed over the clear-cut but tired young faces as he mentioned Agincourt. 'Such losses . . .' began a leisured voice, but with some asperity the old man pushed it aside. 'Losses can never be too high. Never.' His long pitted features wrinkled in contempt. These sprigs, so fascinated by a new scent, designing a new flower, reciting a verse both heathen and shameless, were made speechless not by ambush and array but by mockery, rhyme. They preferred Lyons silk to Toledo steel.

'Our Duke is a skilled warrior, my Lord. And yet he preferred to save many men at Benevento, and chose to lead many back to safety and their mistresses.'

Count Benedict shook his head crossly. Though Simon might conceivably have failings, he was, nevertheless, Duke, and therefore unquestionable and perfect. No more could be said than that he was Duke.

Half in jest, the young men continued to question him. It was fashionable to speak with a slight stutter, another habit that provoked his indignation. Without ostentation, Hode Hunchback had joined them. Only he of them all was aware that, behind that pillar carved with grapes and leering elvish faces, lurked Viscount Charles and Young Roger.

In his rambling yet curiously measured way Count Benedict, trapped into making his favourite speech, was saying, 'Before dubbing, the young squire must clothe himself in brown shoes, to remind himself of that deadly dust into which we all must sink. He must spend the hours before dawn contemplating the Sword. The hilt signifies Christian Fortitude: the edges Loyalty and Justice. Then, hours later, purged by the Bath, surviving the Blow, kneeling for the Accolade, pledging duty to his Lord, and to He who is Lord of us all, wearing a stole of azure, for Chastity, he becomes Knight.'

'And what of Tournaments, my Lord?'

'Tournaments!' His face was seamed with reminiscence. 'I too was a warrior.' Hurriedly he crossed himself and nodded at the Hunchback, whose arm he then struck, to avoid retribution for Pride from that Eye fixed in the exact centre of the universe. 'I was at Charleroi, when only nine lived to tell the day. I was crowned at Châlons. I was at the Rose Joust of the Rhine. It was as if we bore arms in the land of giants. I have carried my lady's veil into the lists, worn it instead of gorgets and have afterwards given it back into her hand stained with my own blood. Surrendering it to her on my lance dripping with the blood of my brother and my foe.'

'Or her girdle, my Lord!'

There were amused nods and several smothered laughs. A slim dark youth murmured, 'I too have my dreams of a Bleeding Lance. Upright!' And the smiles became more open as his companion retorted, 'As for me, last night I had even better fortune.' And they smiled and gesticulated together, like boys rubbing sticks to make a fire, Hode watching intently as Count Benedict retired into his own head, seeing therein long lines of quivering spears and one standard high and gleaming and a young man, so many years ago, kneeling for his Lord's embrace.

'Truth of course, but also vigour,' a youngster had remarked and they chuckled bawdily, swaying their long flimsy sleeves, 'as for me, well, my own Christian courage is like old Eulenspiegel's paintings, invisible to bastards.'

From under grey rigid brows Count Benedict gazed at them reprovingly. 'In Tournament or Combat the Knight rises above himself, he reaches his highest, his rarest Name, he joins hands with God, he acquires for himself Merit by veritably forgetting Self, he reaches his own centre at the very moment of plunging his weapon into the breast of his adversary. He keeps his honour unquestioned and his soul erect.'

At this last phrase they were about to giggle when, from them, but a voice that seemed to speak out of air, belonging to none of them, said in a low thrilling voice:

'Our Lord and Rainault. The White Stag and the Ram.'

They were silent, all recalling that last week Flavius the Nose had foretold that Rainault would vanish entirely within the year.

'But will he come?'

The question was surreptitious, from young Berry, an intimate of the Lord Estrienne's. And at this, Hode grinned into himself and crept away, rubbing his hands at what was so obvious that few dared see it.

Will he come! Count Benedict's brows came further together and his hand unconsciously clutched his grey straight robe. This was the second time that he had heard the question, and it made an ill-omen. The Tournament itself was now only nine days away; nine itself had multiple significance though, in the main, favouring. No definite news of Rainault's arrival had been proclaimed. He had been seen at Adelheim: pilgrims had heard of his sojourn at the monastery of Gault: the Abbot of Linns had sent him a carp: it was rumoured that he had been entertained by the Sicilian Pretender.

They were all interrupted by a shout of fury and Viscount Charles was amongst them, slashing them with his riding switch. His face was bright scarlet. 'Of course he will come!' He swept at them as they dodged and scattered. 'How dare, dare you malign the Prince's word? You rabbits, you millers. . . .'

His hunger or frustration burned so hard on him that they remained still, back, forgetting the switch that had cut their faces and ruined their poses. Their expressions shrank. Only the old Count's features lay firm, sadness falling like a damp mist over his heart, trying to undermine him however much he resisted and set his spurs at it.

With short exquisite bows the young men departed, Charles' glowering eyes following them as, panting, already exhausted, burnt-out, he stood embraced by Young Roger and watched by the foreboding gaze of Count Benedict who, at this moment, seemed part of the old pillar against which he stood.

FOURTEEN

Is he coming? What had hitherto been unquestioned amongst Court and people had been fanned by whispers into a direct question, not always uttered aloud, during the days of Plough Month that preceded Midsummer and the Feast of Saint John. Some too declared that Rainault was secretly encamped outside the walls, that he was preparing to astonish the entire Duchy, that in black vizor and with black shield he was already prowling the streets.

Daily the knights and their retinues were jangling in through the winding lanes and avenues, disregarding the plaudits and exclamations of the citizens, sitting stiff and mailed on their broad muscled horses, flanked by glistening squires.

The ladies, with their costumes completed and lying ready in locked cupboards, were moving about more slowly yet with heightened expressions, caressing each other's bodies lovingly, sometimes withholding themselves from men for a week, a fortnight, then involuntarily capitulating and falling on them with greedy, barely quenchable fervour. They would exclaim, 'The sun, so hot, so smooth', or, 'The trees now, I dream of them every night. In their shade . . . peace, pleasure,' but their eyes, their bodies meant something else, far away, leering, waiting.

The flags were stretched fully as the wind fell lightly over Mars Hill: the tents and pavilions had risen fresh and shining, the grass was green as Glastonbury, the

Lady waited at her Fountain and without startling
resemblance to Isabel who, though expected and invoked,
could not be said to have actually arrived, even if 'really'
she had indeed done so. One by one, and for the last
time, the pledged knights from local manors cantered up to
touch the shields. The most illustrious nobles and errants
delayed their arrival until Midsummer Eve so that not
until the morrow could the real Rainault be expected.

All was now Midsummer Festival. The Duke's dead
father, represented by a priest, lit a fire in the Chapel with
a polished grail. A Red Knight was said to have been
burnt, and another shot in the woods. 'He sees the kind
one,' Flavius murmured everywhere, 'he sees Bel.'

Down in the town the trogeteurs were changing
sparrows into jewels and it was said that slant-eyed men
had ridden in from far borders, men who could behead
you with a special shout and at times restore you with
another. The sky was unbroken, Mary-blue: the Palace
gardens sparkled: parterres were enflamed with roses:
the buffets were filled, water bubbling and edgy in the
sculptured basins. Dressed as Silenus, drunken, half-naked
and merry, the Garden Superintendent capered around
shouting orders to goldsmiths, trimmers, chisellers, who
were adding final splendours to summerhouses that now
rose opulent, domed, bannered, beyond the Orangery,
their rooms designed like chess-boards, river-beds,
grottoes. The Chevalier Stephen had composed a song
praising the birds, for a bird could approach nearer
paradise even than a rider, and, though without souls,
had affinities with children, perhaps the unbaptised. Wise
men who followed the Alençon dukes were already

closeted in the Lord Estrienne's hotel with ingenious disputes about the Holy Seven: the Father, the Sun-Runner, the Persian, the Lion, the Armed One, the Concealed, the Raven: learnedly discussing He Who was born of a Rock under the House of the Ox and the Ass. Into the jewelled ear of the Cardinal-Legate a dark-skinned turbaned figure was whispering the writ of the Assassins: 'Man can behave as he wishes. The stars are dead. All is permitted.' And outside squires and lords were regarding the tall-columned hotels and halls, foreign lords from the Empire with narrow-browed, hollow-looking serfs in leather, light-footed Italians gesticulating at the roof-lunatics, strong hairy Sicilians with armour delicate as if spun, Spanish lords with black followers affecting to see nothing but their own noses. The yellow of Conti marching with the azure and gold-dust of Sidonia and the golden leopards of Anjou.

In the side-streets, under stone balconies, muddy children were dancing and skipping in intricate maze-steps, their high voices chanting as, unawares, they mimed the deeds of forgotten heroes.

> 'Apple jelly lemon a-pair,
>   Golden and Silver she shall wear.
> Gold and Silver by her side
>   Take Lady Isabel for your bride
>   And take her to Troy over lily-white sea.'

Throughout the Capital murmurs, exclamations, plaudits would rise to uproarious heights through the blond sunlight, the splendour thickening until midnight when the cartwheels would be sent blazing downhill in honour

of Saint John, Lord of Oaks, and fireworks scatter the
darkness and mummers enact the Sorrows of Potiphar or
Little John's Pleasures. A bull would be covered with
pitch and set alight. From the University precincts came
the wild chant of students:

> 'The Number Eight singeth the praise with us.
> Amen.
> The Number Twelve danceth on high. Amen.'

All mirrored the dance of the universe, blood singing to
heart, heart leaping at fireworks, fireworks signalling to
the stars to which all human dancers were joined by
myriad unseen threads.

Midsummer Eve, and all must join hands, stamping
and shouting, gripping and thrusting in a vast unending
circle, those of the Duke's household struggling in every
possible posture to exorcise that base thought of Is He
Coming?

The Duke was the natural pivot of the dance though,
were Rainault to be delayed, he would lack a partner and
his own circle would be incomplete. Could he break
what was not? Early that morning in cerise costume and
purple plumes he had led the procession to the Cathedral
for the Mass in honour of Henry the Fowler, founder of
tournaments, the populace briefly awed by the dazzle
of visiting troupes. Alternate coxcomb hoods, and hoods
of the sun in splendour, and streaming gonfalons. The
Blacks and Argents of the Neapolitan, the Medici Red
Balls on Gold Field. The Portcullis of Remy. The White
Stag. The Unicorn-Moon of Saint Gule.

That night there was held a Feast Solemn and Extraordinary. All the bells of the capital pounded and clashed. Having already kissed the Noble Friend, Duke Simon was greeting the Duchess under a canopy woven with 'All Passes' in roses and lilies and flaming dragons'-tongues.

The Duke and Duchess led the way, walking very slowly, preceded by chamberlains bearing gold and silver wands, moving in flaring torch-lit concourse through the State Halls: the Hall of the Birds, the Hall of Gold, the Hall of the Dukes with its blind heroic statues, into the vaulted Feasting Hall itself with the deep golds and crimsons and greens of captured banners. Precedence was most strictly observed, as though a fault in the order would be echoed in the heavens and Orion crash against Perseus, and Jupiter be swung from his own lustrous orbit.

Already, treading in slow measure, escorted by the torch-bearers, with the windows flung open so that the distant, starry sky obtruded between heavy bouts of tapestry and flame, the long procession was within sound of flutes, viols and horns. Hair was being worn high this year, as the last harvest had been poor, and in the wayward, distorting lights the lords and ladies with their towering head-dresses and conical hats, their long pointed sleeves and gloves, their bright upward stripes, their tapering gowns and hose and their lengthy slippers, seemed longer and thinner than they really were. A new race of giants was slowly pacing the Palace, so that the torch-bearers and servitors dwindled and, had the dwarfs been with them, they would have seemed minute and bewitched. The men were wearing short coats quilted with lilies and roses, marguerites and hyacinths, their legs shining to the thigh, their coats slashed and divided. Now their immense shadows struck out weirdly against the tapestries of Guerin the Boar-Killer, the Seven Sages, the Nine Knights and the Nine Amazons, and the flutes and horns spiralled immediately ahead.

Clad in bistre, in rosine, in maroon, sleeves puffed and jewelled, hands powdered, the pages stood behind the chairs of their lords and ladies. The tables, long and curving, were supported by painted eagles, dolphins, minotaurs. Pewter jugs, gold caskets and bowls, silver sticks and knives shimmered above the blackened wood, interspersed with molten figures so heated and intense that the eye could not at once distinguish them. Torches burned from the walls, and on the ceiling gilded birds seemed arrested in flight, their tails filled with jewels.

At certain tables ladies were sitting alternately with men according to the Duke's command, their breasts bare beneath resplendent chokers. Hounds with diamond-set collars curled at their feet. Servants with ballooned sleeves and long chained poulaines held more torches, standing beneath dim heavy tapestries. Count Benedict, in scarlet robes, was greeting old friends and vassals: a Knight of Thomar, a Rhenish baron, the Regent of Osnabruck, an earl from Mary-England.

Trumpets announced the Lord of the Soups, leading the Four Estates of Body and Mouth: the cooks, carvers, cup-bearers and breadmasters. Not yet roused by wine and jest the feasters were already reclining, nibbling ortolans on silver picks, lazily applauding as trumpet and kettle-drum flourished for each dish, borne in on precious platters, first towards the Duke and Duchess seated under red taffeta embroidered with golden griffins, then to be blessed by the Archbishop, saluted by the Cardinal-Legate, then dispensed to the companies. After each course the particular master-cook, standing under an arch, bowed low for the acclamations. Steam rose, mingling with the painted birds that streamed for ever against the shadowy vaulted roof. A diamond, then a griffin's paw, had been dropped into the Duke's wine as a protection against poison; and during this, there were few who did not remind themselves that this might be the last night of Simon's life, and glanced with renewed curiosity at the scorched, tremulous features of his heir.

On such a night the bounty of the Duchy was unstinted. Hot piles of plover and snipe and crane: peacocks roasted in cinnamon, then replaced in their skins and opulent feathers, and served with gilded combs and their eye-sockets set with pearls. Ragouts of capon and squirrel topped with condiniac: sugared mackerel: suckets shaped as unicorns, swans, frogs: neat's tongue pasties: fowls stuffed with currants, sugar, lemon peel, egg and ginger: thick salmon with oranges in their mouths: nuts in sugar icing: pâtés from Perigord and Carcassonne: veal twined with cloves, asparagus and quails' breasts: turkeys rich with stuffed partridges and saffron-pasted ducklings: brawn smeared with goose-liver: hams and pigeon mince cut like delphiniums: beef roasted with cucumber and apple: peaches afloat in Hippocras: sweets flavoured with jasmine, rosemary and marigold: squares of marchpane: flowered custards: towering silver boats carved into dolphins and piled with shell-fish: glittering

cornucopias of fruit: thin trout with silver spray wired
on to blue fins: mitred or centaur-shaped jellies: tinted
flawns: heavy flagons mounted by stone tritons and
titans: a venison hump carved with the Nunc Dimittus
in gold leaf. At the Duke's table live naked boys powdered
with gold stood on pastry-turrets a yard high: giant
chess-men were ranked around a pearled golden elephant
that stood above the feasters' heads. In the centre, reaching over thirty feet above the floor, was a fountain of
flowers gracefully surmounting a White Stag, the flaming
lights making it as though the blossoms were in a
continuous liquid descent, to moisten the ranged flower-
shields of the most ancient and valorous lords present.

In sudden commotion, 'You civet . . . !' Flavius the
Nose chased Hode from the hall, several Rhenish bur-
graves stamping and waving their goblets. A moment
later Flavius, strewn with bells and carrying an ivory
staff entwined with bryony, was back amongst them,
gesticulating as if with a harp and singing, 'By adding
minutes and hours you shorten your life.'

Using his fork as deftly as he might a rapier, the
Chevalier Stephen was speaking quietly to himself so
that no-one should hear. In the gallery musicians were
playing and, after a clarion had imposed quiet, a youthful
voice began:

> 'Swan, and in the river, ghost:
> Ghost, and in the mirror, life.'

All waved and cried out, for the song was the Duke's.
He responded with a salutation, then rose to kiss the
Duchess' hand. Katherine, flanked by the massive

Constable of the Parapets and the Cardinal-Legate, was pale but composed, yellow and blue flowers between her breasts and the heavy coronet of Our Lady of Brey beneath her hennin on which lay beryls and amethysts. Behind her, Flavius, eyes alert for the hunchback to whom he owed yet another blow, was whispering in half-song: 'Be not tempted by the flower, be not beckoned by the dust. She who is out may yet be in. She who is coming may remain out, out, out.' But in an instant an Imperial marquis in greens and reds, wearing on his head-piece a golden cage with a linnet in it, was bending precariously, to kiss her shoulder, mouthing in incomprehensible accents, apparently declaring that she was more beautiful than the day.

Beneath the opalescent Flower Fountain, whose top, now that heads were becoming heavy, it was increasingly difficult to distinguish, various noblemen had made an enclave in the surrounding noise and were gravely discussing Meaning with the Lord Estrienne, at this moment washing his hands in rose-water handed him by a kneeling page, before cutting a queen-apple into thirteen slices, as a gibe against superstition. The stained, bearded face opposite quivered over the wine. If, as the Paymaster General had suggested, there was no Evil, then there was therefore no Good. Morals were but priestly, social or scholastic refinements of the brute essence. Life's aim was fulfilment, either comically or tragically, creatively or destructively.

'The reign of God, of life for the sake of Redemption, is ending. That of the Devil, life for the sake of personal pleasure and carnal satisfaction is drawing nigh.'

117

The Lord Estrienne smiled thinly. He picked at some baked venison. 'Life for the sake of Death is being replaced by life for the sake of Life.' But could most of the lusty fellows escape the terrors of Nothing? Could they escape the Idea of the Thing, the Idea of the Man, and cleave to the Thing in itself, the Man in himself?

'Nevertheless,' a voice objected, 'we are told that the Snake stole for itself the secret of immortality. In the Garden. And, for God's glory. . . .'

'But does the divine glory depend wholly on pageantry? Or can there be true pageantry without God? Does Colour exist where godlessness abounds? In a word, does God depend upon life, or life upon God?'

'What you are asking,' the Lord Estrienne said with his disturbing patience, 'is whether life depends upon life. I would ask your highnesses to consider whether, under the most scrupulous examination. . . .'

Watched by the cool superior eyes of the Duke's favourite lordlings who had previously been jeering at a table of wealthy burghers, batches of elder barons, making themselves clumsy by their refusal to use the newly-imported and probably heathen fork, were gaily toasting Old Times. Wilhelm of Ulm with his one eye; Lully of Lusignan, descendant of a fish-goddess and cousin of the Cypriot king: tusky old Gaston of Montmerial with his frantic voice and ravaged cheeks, demanding pewter instead of glass and grumbling at the presence of lawyers. Old tales abounded between the beards. How the French king and his friends had dressed as Wild Men, with pelts soaked in pitch, and the Duke of Orleans had thrown a torch and five had died in the flames and the

King lost his wits: how Harold Hardrada had shot an apple off his son's head: how Emperor Sigismund, three days dead, sat robed and crowned on his throne so that men might see that the Lord of the World was dead and gone: how Bernarbo Visconti had forced the Papal Legate to consume the Bull of Excommunication, metal seal and all. How Rienzi the Tribune was stabbed before he could make magic with his mouth. How Fulke of Anjou had married a Devil. And how Jacques de Molé, Grand Master of the Templars, dying and agonised at the stake, had successfully summoned Philip the Fair and Pope Clement to meet him within the year before the Judgment of God.

Goaded by the wine and the urgent, pulsing women and the anticipation of the morrow's blood, the talk roamed back and back. To Bohemund of Antioch, Almas, Sir Hector and Sir Bors. Meanwhile Count Benedict was saying severely, 'They are merely rich. They are without honour and they know not dignity,' joining in the condemnation of the disgusting behaviour of that young Armagnac who had killed his sister, not with his own hands but with those of servants.

At the foot of the table painters were watching with greedy, adroit eyes: ostrich feathers, a countess already drunk, her eyes frantic with the lust that had been accumulating through the last weeks, a live mermaid wreathed in green and white sugar, a stream of coloured birds flowing from a pie towards the ceiling, there to join their painted brothers in panic and bewilderment, several dashing themselves against the fretted work and falling senseless to the tables. Simultaneously, the painters were disputing with full throat whether or not this new fashion for landscape meant lack of discrimination, insensibility to form and secrets, mere licence, or a freeing of the soul. Beneath them a voice breathed unsteadily:

'They enjoy being beaten. It proves your love.'

Many had noticed that the Duke was drinking as much as anyone, responding to each toast with an unwonted animation which embraced all but his son, and the Duchess, lonely despite her admirers and retainers.

Voices turned incessantly to the morrow's contests. Foremost of all was Duke Simon's elate and joyous passage of arms with infamous Rainault. Wagers were being laid, concealed by toasts and compliments and praises, pursued by that maladroit whisper of 'Will he Come?'

'I would say that the eye and hand of the Lord Duke are worth a bag of gold and a vineyard facing south.'

'It has been said that Rainault, ever-victorious, should be marked down for a suit of silver armour, a Moorish virgin, an illuminated manuscript of proverbs.'

'It must be remembered that five summers ago, after riding all night, the Prince of Utrecht laid low his several adversaries. Whereas the Lord Duke, mindful, notwithstanding, of his father's arm and his grandfather's knowledge, would not himself claim. . . .'

Many lords had already been practising in the tilt-yards before large experienced crowds. But the Duke's prowess was secret. Not for four years had he borne arms on a campaign: last year in the lists he had conquered with ease, but against no Champion. Eyes swung back at him. Now he was talking rapidly, face flushed, eyes glinting, though once more it was observed that he had not left his seat to embrace the Duchess, who remained, still and sad, making only perfunctory rejoinders to the compliments crowding in on her.

The atmosphere was hot, tinted, uncertain. The festivities gained pace. Many Germans were already drunk, several chewing the flowers, mistaking their purpose. An immense pie, heavily applauded, was served, cut open, revealed three musicians playing the Duke's song. Yet more dishes were in procession. A Golden Ram of sweetmeats. A Chess-cake with figures of gold dust, replacing the powdered boys who, on a plea from the Duchess, had been allowed to jump down and retire. A fleet with rigging and banners all of subtly coloured fish. A sylvan scene made of ice, of Vivien in the green wood with old Merlin asleep at her feet. Two heroes suckled by a wolf, carved from chocolate and strewn with pearls and heliotropes. From one table rose glittering Babel, rising, rising, then collapsing, winged dwarfs capering away while the ruins were transformed into flowers, set in the Duke's motto growing from a march-pane meadow and with bees swarming over them.

Impulsively, the Duke was on his feet, greeted with roars and stamping. He was waving for silence, drinking, to what was it? To the Crusade. So often had he spoken of it, treasuring the plan of it, and now, suddenly, it was real, there, under the moon, waiting. All were standing, applauding, swallowing, drinking, and to the hundreds waiting outside the thick shout heaved up again and again, 'To Jerusalem. Jerusalem.'

FIFTEEN

MIDSUMMER DAY, the year's High Crown. Blue and gold hung deepest as the sky moved to its limit, from the swollen sun that despatched its thousand swift couriers to touch helms, plumes, angles, the metals and jewels moving below as the streets filled and the solid jabbering concourse hurried to the Field of Mars.

Gold: like the blood of kings and lions, an archangel hue supporting all lines and mansions of the universe.

Led by the Margrave of Thuringia, a party of German lords, already armed, was returning from the spectacle of a dog mauled by a wolf, now clanking off to inspect the leopards prowling in the Hubertus Keep. More armoured forms were standing together in the Great Yard while their horses were being accoutred. Momentarily they were silent, staring at a row of cannon pointing outwards towards the city from the grassed Castle slope. This was the Duke's celebrated Iron Family: the Maiden, Long Christ, the Virgin of Tuscany, the Child of Syracuse, the Moor, the Song of Bohemia. Slender, elegant in their chasings, ominous in soundless restraint, they tugged at the eye as if from the other side of a mysterious frontier. Silvery in the sunlight, their intricate scroll-work displayed the death of Dido, the pride of Niobe, Camilla pierced, Sir Tristan beneath a mast, Love Routed, old Charlemagne enthroned. . . . For all their glitter they were solitary, in sinister virginity, always about to thunder, like Jove's sky.

In contrast the lords, transfixed before them, appeared

over-bulky, over-magnificent in their armour: their breastplates, iron inlaid with silver, with gold, were thicker than ever: their helmets, now unvisored, were plumed and lavish: one casque was topped with a green jagged dragon's-wing, another with a golden globe supporting a throne with crimson crown aloft, another was double-turbaned with coils of black and silver. More heads, seen against the sky, stared down, beaked and slitted from beneath golden stags, jewelled lions, wide jagged teeth, dark hammers. Some were as if hard Saracen birds had alighted on their helms. Gussets were of solid Tuscan iron: greaves were burnished as if about to break into flame. Hauberks were threaded with gold. Gold too darted from spears, gloves, sheaves, while the banderoles on lances, upheld by waiting pages hung in scattered peacock radiance. Even the squires' baldrics were thick with flashing stones, as were the swordshafts and casings, wildly, hysterically catching and transforming the light. Enscribed on breast plates were trees, dragons, cities, angry angels, fields of flower and leaf.

The cannons still held and oppressed the high lords while, on the outskirts, hands were pointed at shields and voices murmured famous names. Emblazoned gules confronted sable: slanting purpled lines showed the de Rivay Purpose: vert the Joy of Hesse: the golden Gryphon Sun of Bel Comté.

Finally, with an effort, withdrawing themselves from a mood that might endanger them, the lords slowly turned themselves, awkwardly in their weights, as though in another time. Then, preceded by unfurled pennons, they proceeded through flaunting gardens to where, in Duke's

Meadow, their horses waited. From a grove a sly Hermes mocked. A marble peacock, with fountain-spray for tail, cast empty jewels in their path. Out of the heavy purple blossoms drifted butterflies, Gabriel's Gloves or Thessalian Feathers, spiralling away through the burning illuminated air.

The convolutions and conceits of the headpieces were matched by the twisted shapes of hedge, tree, shrub, and by the endless eyes, limbs, stars, blood-swarms, stripes of the flowers, which in their turn might be expected to breed figures to cousin those so slowly and elaborately stalking to the lists: to breed the flaming chimera and ashy phoenix, the snorting pegasus and massed fumy python.

The smaller fields were crowded with booths, huckster stalls, markets, or set with blue and gold quintain poles or tilting barriers. Around, were stationed the Knights' tents, each with the shield before it and a stationary page. Everywhere the crowds roamed: gypsies with hidden eyes, chattering citizens and their wives: child buyers from sea-ports skilled in the manufacture of eunuchs, hunchbacks and misshapen dwarfs.

The most splendid and illustrious company thronged the green central rectangle, at one end of which was the coloured triangular tent of the Challenger, his personal banner limp overhead and, outside, his shield, quartered white, violet, purple overspread with white tears, and the yellow leopards and White Stag. Opposing, at the end of the smooth, ominous sweep, was the black and white tent, with emblazons and standard of Rainault of Utrecht.

On the third side was the Pavilion of the Lady, with two white blank shields guarded by knights in golden armour, the Fountain plumage making rainbows in the sunlight. Facing this, topped by a silvery image of Venus, Lady of Foam, in the centre of a considerable stand filled with nobility, prelates and the influential merchants, was the Gallery of the Queen of Love and Beauty, presumably, were she indeed present, the Lady Isabel herself, living replica of her waxen sister opposite, so stiff with brocade, so coiffeured with emeralds, and seated in the shadowy arbouret behind the Fountain.

Mantled with love-entwined roses, unicorns and dying gods was the Throne, still empty, blue and green trumpets dangling around it on shining wires and to which, wide and expectant, thousands of eyes continually turned.

The lords were riding on solid caparisoned horses between packed cheering banks of onlookers. There was much laughter as the populace singled out Wilhelm Van der Merk, the wealthiest merchant in the Duchy, who rode with them, uninvited, clad as a knight. One rider, with an immense shield and dazzling plume, was so overladen that he toppled and fell, to the delight of the groundlings and the shrewd cackles of those soberly gowned merchants, massed as if for security in their gallery, amid the silks and fashions of the nobility, their eyes, slow and thoughtful, watching everything.

Voices of lesser quality were identifying the various bannerets.

'There . . . the double eagle. Habsburg. Young Joseph himself.'

'The Marquis. The Black Lion of Flanders.'

'The Tusked Yale of Beaufort.'

To shouts and applause a trumpet sounded and three Marshals, all flaunting the Silver Centaur standing on Black Rock, rode together down the turf saluting the throne, streamers from their helms flowing out behind them. Two heralds preceded them on grey palfreys. More trumpets; then, speeding together, the heralds dismounted beneath the Gallery and, in high monotonous chorus, called upon the most exalted princes Rainault and Simon, Simon and Rainault, to appear in arms forthwith so that God Avenger might defend the right.

A mot was called, the notes climbing one after another like jugglers' balls, strangely held, then descending in a whole. In reply, shrill and silvered, came further notes, ending in sudden and spontaneous acclamation for the solitary rider now seen at the Challenger's end. A slight balanced figure in pale grey armour, pleated steel skirt, lance pointing downwards, black plume erect, was moving forward smoothly, as if gliding, on a shining roan upon whose dull-gold champon the spike burned hard and single. It was the Duke: his head, utterly covered, ironed, was blank and inhuman, bird-like, encased in its grilled burgonet. Behind him with a spare lance rode a squire.

The Duke's riding was exact, perfect as a rose brought to full fledge and thus already on the verge of dissolution: like a song reaching finest pitch and briefly suspended while the listeners sensed and even experienced the passing of centuries. Reining, he made the half-turn with the accustomed motions and sat, composed and square, his lance now pointed level, facing the narrow lengths ahead.

Silence, until a further trumpet, parody of that harsh and curious blast that had croaked from the sky on the first day of the century. A roar, as if falconets had thundered, and for one instant all felt that here at last was Rainault, defiant and vulnerable. But it was only the call of the Minor Marshal uttering the Second Warning.

The space before the black and white tent remained empty. The emptiness, watched by the parched, exclamatory eyes, was patent, inescapable, an entity from which monsters were born and gods seen. But voices were already murmuring in tidal rage. Rainault had but one last moment in which to appear. Was he a mere braggart, a carpet knight? Or had perhaps his witch exhausted him?

The pale grey Duke remained as if carved, ready to hurl down all knights from each corner of the world and attracting all hearts, though, from his place in the Mounting Yard, Charles was staring at him with waiting intensity, as if attempting some ambiguous enchantment.

Amid such breathlessness the Third Call rose, wavered, lost itself in heat and growls and a long wail of disappointment.

Watching with charred, skilful eyes the Lord Estrienne noticed the jealousy settling, scarcely awares, on the red jowled features of the prelates at his side. Tournaments, he reflected to his companion, a scented graceful youth, were rudimentary metaphors initiating you into more secrets than that which awaited all who knew not the

Name, secrets more dramatic and indeed more plausible than those hinted at by priests.

The Duke, alone on the green, had opened his visor. As he spoke the squire moved up.

'Has the Lord Rainault come?'

'Yes, my dear Liege.'

'But his trumpet is silent.'

'It is about to sound.'

'Yet I hear nothing.'

'He is still on the road.'

'I think he is far away.'

The young man lowered his head. His voice was low, troubled, shamed. 'He has crossed no frontier to-day, Your Grace.'

A full moment of acclamation and alarums was followed by a supreme void as Rainault's standard was lowered: some said that it should be trampled on, a great number hooted derisively. The Duke, after his ovation, had withdrawn.

Soon, in the various fields, the general jousting and tilting had begun. Banners streamed out, orange and black, scarlet and green, quartered and divided. Ladies tossed down scarves, kerchiefs, embroidered squares to their champions. The Duchess entered the Queen's Gallery, in state, to sit enthroned on a seat hung with panther skins. Countess Isabel dwindled to a minstrel's rhyme: a ghost.

Scrutinised by that meditative and even cunning gaze of the robed, opulent merchants, many combatants, weighted by armour too heavy, too gorgeous, collapsed and could not rise. They lay on the sward, writhing and helpless, squires rushing to assist, for that interval their nobility becoming kin to the freaks and exhibits at fairs and markets.

At one period the Wild Boars were taking on all comers, Viscount Charles laying about him with a mace, in ferocious and maddened escape from the limitations of the Palace. Subsequently there was a mock passage-of-arms between Flavius the Nose and an ape tied to a pony. Hours later, as the last frenzied notes of sunlight fell on the lopped casques, shattered horses, lost plates and broken plumes, wild crowds saw the Duchess with crown aloft standing to receive the Victor, Gervaise of Anjou, who had seven times struck the attaint and who now laid his garland at her feet. Flayed by blood and arms the entire city seemed applauding, but within the good cheer was much weeping and grief as people gazed past the fallen shapes, past the dense brooding outlines of knights, to where earth and sky joined in common defeat as the sun splintered and darkness obtruded and the inner voice muttered beneath the howls of mirth, victory, festivity:
    'He did not come.'

SIXTEEN

THE Duke was in his private turret enthroned before a mirror. Grey-blue eyes looked back at him from above their faint irrevocable scroll-work of lines.

On small ivoried tables and escritoires were his chessmen, kept alive since Babylon by inexplicable potency: also the playing cards, the clocks, the books of mottoes and riddles, all with their secret existences, caught up, thrown back, enlarged by the painted mirrors, as it were rebounding.

Had he really expected Rainault? He sighed. There had always been so many questions, ever since that day, years ago, when he had been puzzled at being forbidden to sleep under trees at noon. By an old, nameless nurse who had eventually been hustled away, screaming, with all her hair shorn, and never seen again.

Childhood questions but even now never fully answered, accumulating new meanings through the years. Would a river *feel*? Could music *live*? On the other side of music, *what*? Why must dukes sometimes limp? Suppose you slept and never awoke? Or touched a priest with your left hand! Always that weird nausea at left-handedness. Grandfather, with his magic spiders and silent furies, the terror of priests and robbers, who had closeted himself with lode-stones and mandalas, collected raven-stones for invisibility and understood birds' speech through allowing his ears to be licked by the Snake, he had had twins and the left-handed slain. It was said in the Palace that a left-handed baby Robert would have become

Duke but for this, so that for young Simon certain passage-ways, certain shadows, certain turns of the way were unpleasantly haunted, and in certain moods he felt a gap in himself, hollowed out by the accusing stare of his lost brother.

As a small boy Simon had imagined that 'other people' were part of himself and, becoming a man, he had wondered whether animals thought this, so that thus all men began as animals and many remained so. The Lord Estrienne had always maintained that humanity was not born with a soul but developed one only through unusual challenges though, as the Archbishop had objected, was it not rather man's possession of a soul that enabled the challenges to be found?

Simon, Duke, pondered these matters. The White Stag was emblem of the House, so that, whatever the properties of the soul, in queer ill-defined transition, Dukes and their sons were themselves animals.

Childhood days: how tall he could be, tall as the French King who, jabbering about ghosts, had come that blue afternoon to hunt: how too he had soared with that bird: or tottered with mouldy old Countess Bird's Nest. Then become an armoured shoe shaped like a lobster-claw.

Awaking, as the sunlight slides into the room, the boy gradually adjusts himself to all the motionless objects that have survived the night. Surely, however, that Chess-King has moved three squares, and shoes have crossed the floor and the room itself has dwindled during the furtive, murderous hours of darkness! Later, the games in the courtyard with pages and squires,

Stephen dressed as a bull and the dwarfs capering and jingling, making you forget' the lepers and cripples crouching at the gate and the thigh-bone of Saint Louis in the Fleece Closet, and those dances that are forbidden and the high uncanny hourglass in the Zealand Gallery. At table platters and goblets are always laid for 'Robert' as though it is not only his ghost that remains, waiting on stairways, on battlements.

On becoming Duke, Simon had announced 'Robert's' death, the Duchy had mourned three weeks, and a funeral procession of over a mile had paraded the capital, and a silver coffin been buried under the royal altar in the Cathedral.

War had been a word filling those early days. The front rank was always moving forward: was it not possible, Simon had once asked, to station oneself in the second rank? In alarm he had recoiled at the shocked eyes and lips of Count Benedict: as though he had exposed a secret.

Duke Simon gazed into the mirror. In childhood, before acquiring the chilled face of Dukes, he had, every morning, set his 'face for the day'. Melancholy like the painting of Prince Alain who had vanished into seas, smiling and terrible like grandfather, laughing like Stephen, gentle as mother, whose ancestors had been dove-begotten. Now, however, his face must remain identical throughout the year: smooth, controlled, promising nothing.

Feast Days occurred, profound strokes and impressions cut into the year; Candlemas with its white tapers and snowdrops; Easter all gold and green; Lammas, with peasants dancing the Corn-Baby; Michaelmas, when the Duke presented geese to the burghers.

Simon had imagined that a certain birthday would renew his life, give him a secret name, answer all questions, but he did not know on which year this would befall. Meanwhile he tried again and again to kiss his forehead in the mirror, thus to grow a horn and live for ever. There was also his shadow and his fear of it being trapped and stamped upon by 'enemies'. But stamp on it yourself, kill it and fling it away and you overcome that grievous knight, Sir Death. Old Nurse Feeble, up in her turret, was whispering of Dietrich the Bold, seen by men for over three hundred years and whom Simon had himself seen at some feast, Dietrich who moved in full sunlight yet cast no shadow.

To remain still was not permitted. His father's councillor, Count Benedict, was already teaching him to assess Colour. Each colour had its heraldic meaning, contradicted though this might be by its religious or, yet again, by its moral meanings. Green, the Duchess' colour, was never so green as might be supposed, confusing Lady Mother with the fertility of fields, or with Envy. And Duke's sons were simultaneously purity-white and Caesar-purple. Similarly, Mother was not always 'mother'. At special times of the day she became 'Your Grace', at signal periods of the month merely 'Her'. Eventually she was 'The Good Duchess' and finally nothing at all, a patch of dark air in the vast Sarcophagus Ducorum decorated after Milano.

All was entangled by what his tutor, the Lord Estrienne, would term 'appearance', by which everything was no more than a revelation of something else, without which it could not be understood. Thus to-day the New Art was scandalising the old men, who could not be expected to agree that Green might be nothing more than green.

The Lord Estrienne spoke more often of money-handling and the needs of councils and princes than of Colour and the House of Aries. Particularly he discoursed of wool, so that at times the Duchy seemed no more than a giant Lamb feeding upon itself. Young Simon listened, nodded, thought much.

His body too was stirring, his sex had moved and, throughout, his father was teaching him to wear pride like armour, and Mother, in that hour before she resumed Grace, told him that, like God and His sons, he was different. In his honour the Knighthood of the Masque Vert was being instituted, with its heralds and chapels, its anagrams, oaths and passwords.

Simon he was, and he wondered what further name he would be awarded by the people. Simon the Good, Simon the Terrible, Simon Lackland, Simon the Great, Black Simon. Each suggested a new and singular posture. The people possessed this solitary power over rulers, this endless bestowal of names, names to be repeated and considered by men not yet born. Old Benedict, old and tufty even then, had told him of Simon Magus who had flown before Lord Nero: Simon Peter whom God had cursed yet chosen: Simon Zealotes who had 'known' God: Simon Cyrene who had carried the Cross: Simon the Earl, who had battered to death the dancing South.

Subsequently, the Lord Estrienne had taught him the

true significance of a name, though most names apparently meant nothing at all or could be chipped down to one Name which was either not thoroughly understood or had been forgotten. In transit, however, names revealed certain ephemeral meanings which it was the duty of princes, prelates, masters to understand, then keep to themselves. A thing is, yet is not, like the bend of a stick thrust into water.

Young Simon listened profoundly though, within him, uncovering perhaps a further name, an additional colour, a voice had spoken of 'Wild Lands' and father, at this moment not father at all but the Lord Duke, might exclaim as if enchanted, 'The Crusade', that stupendous energy which was always just about to happen. To see the gorgon in the lightning cloud and hear the siren in the wind: to voyage beyond Urbino with its thirteen towers, London with its boy-beaters and warring nobles, to sail beyond Africa and Tyre, on such impulses were the Wild Lands built, calling for Crusades.

Often there was talk of Frontiers. He had stood on battlements to see his father ride out with long trains of men-at-arms, his knights around him like dark clanking forts. How pale the Duchess had looked, at once dissolving into 'mother', wet with tears and her arms loving. Father was defending his Name and, on his return in rainy autumn, there had been bells, banners, wagon-loads of treasure and wounded, and names were more resounding than ever.

Now a new delight swarmed up, out of the air. Because of Katherine, dancing by herself, grave and alone, yet laughing, surmounted by light. And he was ready, like a bow bent at full tension. What kissing they had had, what plunging and tears in the woods, what ecstasies by the river, what white dreams, what chansonettes of death and sacrifice, what hunts, what riding through air, what love. He still trembled with lust as he thought of it. Unexpected as Pan, recollections would trap him: at Confession, at Council, at Mass, in a joke about seals chanting psalms off the Western Islands. Easy old Chaplain Van Meeg with his eleven bastards would forgive him that. He and Katherine had exchanged souls, knowing each other's thoughts, knowing when each was dreaming of the other, sharing blood. Yes: he could open heart to wind and sky, to vagabond dust and the pool.

Striding alone in woods, then lying down undefended, falling asleep, Simon the Heir, Third of the Dukes, had dreamed of a sword in the earth. Sweating, crying aloud, he had awoken: the forest was soundless and still, wrapped in bright queer intensity of light that turned the spaces between leaf and twig into eyes, drew down the hot sky, turned breath into warnings. Moved by half-dreaming will he had knelt, tearing at moss and grass and earth, frantic for discovery, finally in terror and triumph uncovering a grey flat stone, faded and cracked and disconsolate but with a single word dug into it, deep as time and perhaps as fearful. He spelt it out, savouring it aloud, fearful of being overheard, hurriedly crossing himself as he pronounced it in utmost strength, caught back in the power of the virgin body bricked up in the chapel wall.

He knelt, his forehead touching the cold, damp stone and he whispered:

'Attila.'

In the Palace Father, the Duke, was ageing. Already he had given his son blood-blessing. Again and again he repeated, 'A Duke, a King, goes with his head in the air. As Above, so Below, the Ancient Men said. Listen well to the Lord Estrienne but preserve your own counsel.'

Once a year, before the entire court, his father's titles, revenues, possessions were proclaimed anew: for this day it appeared that the Duke was Lord of the Empire, King of Arles, Regent of Scotland, Archduke of Lorraine: that England and Bohemia were his vassals and that he was Lord Protector of most of the coffers, manors and walled cities on this side of Trebizond and bulging Asia. And now Simon the Heir, for some forgotten reason pretending to limp, was being initiated as Master of the Cordwainers' Guild, as Lord Provost of Hévres, as Knight Supreme of Trèche: he was wielding a lance, receiving a holy relic of Theophylact the Intolerable. Also he was travelling, having first been most strictly instructed that, once across frontiers, he must never refer to the Duchy by its name. Also, when eating strange food, he must cut it into three, in honour of the Trinity.

War came again and his father won a resounding and personal victory, charging the dishonoured at the head of his knights. To young Simon it could never be sufficiently repeated that the conquered provinces were held together by the House alone.

Nevertheless, even beneath the ordered, bustling capital and the magnificence, there were shadows: in dreams no gold could repel the faceless leper, or the tall man with tiny useless arms, or the Templars who had worshipped a Head, or the superb ruler toppling, dragged down to be trampled on by brutal, impassioned feet.

Sometimes he attended the Council, robed and mailed at his father's right hand. Could anything really happen as a result of these mouthings and arguments, were they more than Mass in the Cathedral, a design to humour 'the people', and sign to God that bodies were busy and therefore good? Or more than a bridge, a decorative and perhaps artful addition beneath which the river flowed natheless? Argument never vanquished that talk of 'Frontiers', those whispers of 'Robert' who had been made to vanish.

Katherine could tell him nothing of this. She too was growing up, standing tall and complete in her new black robe with pearls sewn all over her, and her smile set as if in wax as she moved dreamily towards him at the Citizens' Ball. He did not know her. He bowed: he spoke: she nodded: he found that he had nothing to say. She had vanished, danced away leaving behind this effigy. Her soul had wandered. She was not what he had intended.

The Duke and the Lord Estrienne, Count Benedict and the Archbishop had all explained very precisely what the Lady Katherine was. Dramatically and damnably she was transformed, diminishing into rolls of parchment. The Lord Estrienne was discouragingly explicit. She was nineteen castles, she was the left bank of the Meuse, she was the seven windmills of Mayence, she was fifteen thousand gold crowns. How strange that all these had been secreted in her slender body when, only last year, they had stripped each other in grass by the river and found pleasure. His only instant of conviction of God, his union with the Other, the culmination of the dance, the tragic but delicious ecstasy of horns as the mort sounded over the dead, still quivering stag. Now however she was the most revered Lady Katherine and he could not linger. Already he was galloping away as the horn sounded and the hounds bayed and the ghostly cavalcade raced for 'Wild Lands', to Gotholonia, Vandalusia, Arragant and the Land of Castles; his father already ahead, for when you were Duke you rode on and on, swerving neither to left nor right, until you died that the land might live. Katherine and he had tossed the ball of pleasure but, masked by law and a golden crown, the nymph in her would never lead him to 'Wild Lands'. Now the talk was of the Crusade, and, in the wind, drifted murmurs of 'the West' that, like an incantation, like stories of a boar in the mountains, incited the heart. Notwithstanding, he had paced with her down the massy Cathedral, placing the magic on her finger and slaying his love, while the shining ponderous lords and ladies bowed heads and, in white cloud, the virgins stood singing, all dressed in resemblance to Katherine, to confuse devils.

The light dancing spirit had vanished for ever, or disguised herself so thickly that, though he might meet her daily, he would not see her. Confronted by ghosts of that dead summer, he felt as though he had looked upon an archangel and been smitten with blindness, or consumed. Was it that God Immanent had been using Katherine for a message: that the 'real' Katherine had been withdrawn and that now in her place was God himself: and that he and God were in complicity, with God

testing him for a further and colder purpose but one
which had never been vouchsafed? Was it indeed lawful
to love one's wife? The Fathers had held it a sin, though
Chaplain Van Meeg might wink and look around for his
goblet and talk about this dead Katherine as Mary's
Ward and therefore fit and indeed requisite for Christian
Love.

In bed with her, tempted by her ghost, under carved
swelling heads and eyes of elaborate monsters and heroes,
he rode to ecstasy almost as before, but lust should give
more, should transmute, should become, should survive
into morning and solidify the day. Where was treasure,
what was it? The ancient sentences had promised more.

Deus, per quem mulier jungitur viro, et societas
principaliter ordinata, ea benedictione donatur, quae sola
nec per originalis peccati poenam, nec par diluvii est
ablata sententiam.

He was twenty. His wife was the fairest of mortal
women: court poets assured him that she was a raven, a
lily, a sigh from the night, a perfume from the east, an
April morning. Such beauty was as aggravating as
conscience. Could he but find the girl Katherine. The old
Duke his father swayed from hall to hall lamenting his
dead Duchess who had faded with the Old Year, drifted
away like the last note of music played from past days.
Simon wept, mourned, prayed for her in all her mani-
festations, and discovered Sir Death amongst so much
that was black and old and monstrous. Man-lovers bound
together and drowned in the marshes: Host-desecrators
branded and flayed: poisoners and traitors smashed on
the slow appalling wheel: thieves collected and hanged

in batches at a sign from the Duke: trespassing lepers scalded with molten lead. Sin, sin was evident and perhaps, as Count Benedict feared, would overload the world which would then topple over, dragging moon and stars after it. Yet God himself, fashionable light-flavoured voices assured each other, had become a matter of ceremony and mutual respect. And there had been the Lord Estrienne's celebrated disputation with the Archbishop, maintaining that there must be sin in God too, for had he not created all?

In laughter at Hode, at Flavius, at the apes, you could become them, as you became a Chess-king, a victor, a saint, and thus invulnerable. Revolting against splendid apparels, you could retreat to a certain empty and forgotten stone closet and in delightful peril mutter, 'Attila'. Or gaze in gardens at pale statues ready to give homes to all pleading, wandering souls. Or sit alone with cards and chess, clocks and mirrors, in a spare angular world with your being filled with Whither and What and where nothing penetrated but your own misted sensations that struggled and groped. And no-one knew, neither old Benedict, grained like wood and with wise ways, nor Jew Plate, he of the crabbed eyes and clever hands, nor doctors with their crucibles and blades, texts and incantations; nor even the Chevalier Stephen with his experience of other worlds 'beyond the air', of music, painting, shrewd rhymes that settled in the brain like elves and allowed no rest.

Many tournaments were held: aspects of Mars. At sixteen he had fought his first. How often he had watched the shock of arms, the blood, heard the cries of ladies.

felt the horses' thunder. Suddenly he was himself mounted, his hand welded red-hot on the lance, his nerves and eyes rigid, both seeing and not seeing the dark, too thin figure a hundred ells away, armoured and faceless, about to charge and ram. Oh the terror of meeting that wicked point, of being flung down in one vile and terrifying blow, of lying headless and broken on the grass. Already the trumpet had sounded, and as if involuntarily he was speeding towards his challenger, who was rising, rising out of whirling dust, now vast, with all the ponderous inevitable power of a storm blocking the sky. His own hand scalded, his brain had petrifed. Who was watching now? Of itself the horse swerved slightly, there was an extraordinary and fearful collision and he was galloping on and on, he had survived, was Victor, and his blood cried aloud and his spirit swept aloft. But that terror, that evil instant! And in battle: he was on the right wing, royal. The bows were lifting, the arquebuses aiming, now the trumpet would ring, signalling to Death.

At another time all the Palace hounds were baying and moaning and he knew that his father was dead.

Katherine was on her knees before him. All windows were opened to allow the soul to escape. Mirrors were covered and 'the people' were laughing and singing, afraid that lamentations might injure the spirit in its flight.

All night Duke Simon sat by his father's naked exposed body, one candle at the dead man's head, the heavy black draping relieved only by a square of blue for immortality. Hours passed, he sat still as an adder-stone. In a trance.

A fish-god was leading him through darkened halls until he met a youth in a blue robe surrounded by burning swords. And on a wall a bull's head, antique yet freshly severed. Here was descent into Hell: at hand was the Devil, tempting him to be glad of his father's death.

He had said prayers over the old Duke's sword, banner, ring, for fear that they might still be alive and that the ghost needed them. Had the Duchess been alive she would have had to lie four months in her lord's bed, but already that had been removed and burnt.

Now he was Duke. The touch of magic in him swelled and became entire. Or seemed to. The Stag of Righteousness had been seen, roaming in the wind as it always did at a new reign. The House was still preserved.

The 'Wild Lands' were receding. There would be no Crusade next year. Occasionally, tempting music could be heard. From where? From the air, from a hidden room, from his soul or star, or perhaps from some secret residue of Katherine that still lingered, to nag, and promise him the past.

He was enthroned, listening to innumerable voices. The Papal Legate, shrewd as a Prussian, was expounding the treachery of the Visconti. Scotsmen were arguing whether the whirlpool were fish, devil or natural habit. Katherine, who still did not understand that she had deceived herself and become false, was smiling, urging him to dance, to give bounty to the poor, to reward the poor man who had trudged thirty miles to sacrifice to her a carp that he had caught. Her kind heart was as troublesome as her beauty. And the Chevalier was discussing a metrical scheme with a Provençal Wanderer. Yet all

143

sounds were as tiny as those of a hawking bell. Dazed, Simon heard himself giving orders, revoking decisions; then saw himself walking in state with Katherine to the Cathedral, that storehouse of old and spectral shadows, with the very sky raining gold. He wanted to retreat, hide: sit alone in a stone cell with strait vase-paintings, with ice, or to lie listening to virginals in the twilit Hall of Chests. He had his own thoughts as he sat in Council, at Mass, as he marched or rode, knelt or swam or broke the deer or lay confused beside Katherine in the bed, rebuking himself for seeking her, yet gratified by her response and catching fire from it. The most violent and magnificent kings were those who had never existed: ancient lords who hanged themselves on trees and begged to be pierced with spears. By sacrificing yourself to yourself you became Another. But who? At supper there had been the most interesting talk: a real ruler, the Archbishop had maintained, was he who had reached his spiritual centre or, as the Lord Estrienne interpreted it, achieved the seventh understanding. The spirit has many mansions, he said, with his secret smile. The Lord Estrienne, surely almost a heretic, could explain the meaning of life as smoothly as he did that profitable system of Double Entry. That a Persian had been born of a Rock in a cave under the stars and been worshipped by a shepherd. When Satan the Creator destroyed the world the Persian would return and awake the good to new life. Yet all men by right action, right posture, could become the Persian.

It is all very difficult. Was life indeed evil? He sighed, considering again those sights that injured. The drooling eyes and black forced tongues of those hanged for hunting the wren. The dance maniacs terrified of pointed shoes and the colour Red. The Plague Maiden with her fork and black streaming hair. Where was she now? And Bishop Adrian the Beloved, devoured by dogs. Life was shedding petal after petal to reveal the bold bare stump. Wolfgang had dressed as a bull and you ran after him taunting and waving and simple. But years ago there had been an island, proud and labyrinthed, until threatened by earthquake, and gradually that terror became a bull which could be tamed and chained, and the children gibed at the bull and were free.

Contemplation of animals, possession of them, pursuit of them made you free. When you stormed over the earth in the hunt feeling the horse respond beneath you, sensing the power in those tracks in the dust, sensing the blur on the sky-line and the blood within.

His memory at times splintered. Was he changing back into a dog? Happiness was fulfilment, but fulfilment was Death. If Death meant Happiness was it not better to be Unhappy? Such questions trudged at the heel and allowed no grace. Again, if he left the Duchy, would statues of himself thereby begin to feel, thus depriving himself of some sensation and power?

Now for fifteen years he had been Duke. To 'the People' he was greater than all others, therefore to God he must be smaller. These divisions, these clefts! How satisfied he was at women's submission, how contemptuous of their formality, how grieved at their inability to 'see' him, how angry if they succeeded. They too were disguised: let the frontiers be crossed, let Judgment come, and for all their paint and silk they would be no more than peasants of years ago, destroying clocks and crying that they would live for ever.

No frontiers had been crossed. He was Duke. Battles were well enough, but he must teach his son that, while there was a time for attack, there was also a time for retreat. Also, indeed, a time for refraining from fighting. In fashion was a way equally Roman: a dagger spotted with Syrian poison, a single armed emissary knowing just where to strike to earn his reward. By such means you remained Duke, with splendour, largesse, missilia ringing across listening Europe. Pageants grew. Stand on the curved balcony of the Hôtel de Ville and watch, throughout four hours, the execution of the Master of the Rosy Cross. Pack the Field of Mars and watch the Grand Tournament held in honour of beautiful idyllic Isabel.

Katherine, despite her obedience and, as he hoped, suffering, had made no submission: she preserved her frail but unmistakable singularity, receiving poets, warriors, priests with the same subdued but persistent interest. With a sudden hint of jealousy he hastened into another part of himself.

Katherine and he had not aged. In strange wordless ballet they were accompanying each other through this short life. Standing together beneath the Tapestries of Touraine, with hovering poets comparing her to a goddess, the moon, the sky; to flowers, God's favours or Our Lady's secrets, part of him wanted her, wanted to talk with her as in former days, to ride together through an empty night. But that would be to return, to acknowledge that youth was both past and future but never now: that the Wild Lands were abandoned and the search surrendered. To return would be final: a lid closing down, a tree falling. Understanding that she was waiting, he cursed and was tempted to bow down to her . . . that low, oddly stirring voice, those loving yet independent eyes . . . and all at once he hated her. *She knew too much.* She had seen moments when he had not been fully Duke and when he wanted to forgive her, he could not meet her eye, and part of his soul froze.

Charles' career, tainting her, moved her still further off. That she grieved over their son he knew, though they never spoke of it. And now, this last year, he had reached a last isolation, was leagues from her and could exchange no sign.

It was more fruitful to turn from Katherine to the Duchy, with its walled shining cities, its spacious champaign and curving rivers, its tolls and guilds, its soaring balconies and clashing, haunted bells: its great bales of carded wool, the expensive ships poised at river mouths.

Once a year, assisted by Count Benedict, he trapped Charles into challenging him in the lists and with what mingling of defiance and glory he overthrew him, year after year, maintaining his Name. Only this year Benedict's praise had for the first time troubled him. 'At Your Grace's age . . .' and his nerves had gone blank and cold.

People were saying that Charles had been praying nightly for Rainault to avenge him and thereby make him Duke.

I am Simon, I see all. I do not have to use the secret rooms that my grandfather, ever suspicious, ever afraid,

147

had had built into the Palace. Who knows better than I the bribes paid by the Guilds to the Estates General, by the maîtres to the judges, by legatees to the Court of Requests? In my Palace the contractors intrigue with the master-cooks: even the Colleges conspire with livery-men, chamberlains, grooms, like men in the cheaps selling narwhal-bones as unicorns' horns, and coral against enchantment. Such customs, such corruption if you like, protect lands against the frozen law of the Mongols, the Turks, the Bulgars. They maintain flow. A pupil of the Lord Estrienne realises how morals are conditioned by Time. Better to be a sinner after the Incarnation than a virtuous friend of Plato. What is virtuous after harvest is sinful before Lent. To kill a Moor merits Paradise, to kill a Burgundian entails Hell. What is permitted under Pope Innocent is damned under Pope Urban. All passes.

With patience and grandfather-wiliness people can always be mastered. You wait and smile and wait further, until, with a false look, an oblique word, they stutter and fall and become of little account. Very occasionally, an hour of torture, a certain impulse towards stripping, a blood-urge for revenge, a special glance through the grille of the Snake, the Pitiless, the Strangling, those dampest and most fatal dungeons, is allowed to a Duke. From blinded nightingales come sweetest songs.

An assiduous listener at the Council, his authority never questioned, Duke Simon signed the edicts for which he felt little concern. To move 'the People' you had to 'be' a Duke. By his anointed act of being he

148

moved more hearts than all the legislations of Mother Church and Father Council and the lawyers of Bologna and Paris. Simply, no Duke must forget or forgo his own magic, and lose himself in the labyrinth of the common day, though the Tempter was always at hand: in the tennis play, hovering above the heads of chess-men, in stables and gardens, in the trance and beauty of the New Paintings that the Chevalier brought him. The beauty of solitary and commonplace figures approaching from an alley, held in sunlit isolation in a courtyard or under an arch. They beckoned the watcher to run from palaces and gaze at clear shining landscapes all empty and endless: or at an aloof page, an enraged cripple, an unknown and mysterious lord, a wild and incomprehensible preacher, or a singer: masked, fleeting, never to be known. By jerking a shoulder, by trembling a wrist, these strangers pulled you deeper into life, helped even Dukes to persist. They were like controlling characters in masques who from love or hate pretend to be statues.

Within the Palace were too many smiles, too much weariness, too many games. How tiring Stephen actually was, how tedious indeed to have a Noble Friend, expecting to be kissed and fondled. Sleeping alone you could thus spite the flimsy world.

In such a mood the Duke could see how all were fettered: by misuse of words which, the Lord Estrienne declared, contaminated life: by the deep yet cloudy sentences of priests: by memory, foresight, fear, all of which stunted and prevailed. Only in that naked river-moment with Katherine had he 'seemed' utterly free, of rule and time and recollection, and, however wild the hunt, however tormenting the music, he had never regained it.

What did he really want? To declare himself a King? For, though all passes, kingship is fertilised by the years. He did not know. Women's bodies were continually thrusting themselves between him and routine, yet, because he was Duke there was no hunt, no chase: they opened for him at once, he could find no passion for them, the 'real' them. What remained? A last glimpse of the Wild Lands, the lingering possibility of the Crusade next year? Weasels and rue were already being collected, with which to disarm the monstrous desert Basilisk.

The mirror startled him then, gibing at the first greys in his hair and thus in his soul. If destiny was due to one's face, his own had reached its limit. But this waiting, this inaction had become intolerable. He was enclosed: why could not Katherine help him? He must strike out, ride away, overcome.

In a library, gazing at the pallid oval features of some English queen with its crippled eyes and jewelled hair, the Duke had said aloud, out of nothing, 'Isabel', and, with magic, realised that he was now holding the key to the gate through which to ride away, ride away. To the Grail, the Blessed Isle, the West. An intruding and unnecessary thought reminded him that the Noble Friend had once said that, were lands ever to be found there, however wild, however enchanted, the West would then cease to haunt. An 'Isabel' however must be found, at once, before the gaunt mutter of 'Too late'.

Duke Simon had summoned Count Benedict and ordered him to find a noble and veritable Isabel and, when the letters arrived from Trévers, his blood had thrilled and he knew that he was younger. There must be an embassy, gifts, magnificence. A Betrothal: a portrait. Let Katherine know, and weep. Now he had unique power: let old dry Capet in Paris behave himself, let those hogs on the Rhine keep their highways free, let the Emperor himself keep due respect to our most ancient and glorious lands where the ruler swerves neither to left nor right and where, in the woods, lay 'something' of Attila, the damned, the Scourge of God.

Afterwards, recapitulating the excitement, came rumours of Prince Rainault, solidifying into a fact. Betrayal. Men's mockery, all Europe laughing, Charles howling like a dog and tearing tapestries, carpets, fabrics, and felling Young Roger as if to blind him.

New Tournament was ahead, his own Combat, his fire to be quenched or renewed. There, before the multitudes, in the climax of arms he could storm from prison, still with 'head in the air', assume the Persian, cut open the circle.

The Tournament. Who could not notice how roused the women had become during the last weeks, as if feeding their cheeks and bellies on anticipation of blood, holding themselves together by the thought of battle? An expectation echoed, now fully, now faintly, within himself, yearning for display. That music-call as he hurled Charles broken and anguished to the dust. Isabel and Katherine would see him crush Rainault like-wise. Did tournaments rise from a bloody and desperate Sacrifice?

Daily he greeted Katherine, so stiff in her robes, eyes

wide and calm against his courtesies, though locked within her was the girl, merry and friendly, leading him to lie with her by the water. Almost alone of the Palace ladies she was now remaining unperturbed. Perplexed, he wanted to know what she was thinking, of this possibility of his own overthrow and death. Let her not conceive that she would win fine freedom: he would leave orders that she should be sent to a convent, and he smiled, knowing her fear of shaven nuns. But he wanted to know. And, at the back of himself, he realised that she would never wish him ill. And was irritated thereby. Though he tormented her she would always forgive him, not only from bounden duty but from nature.

'We hear heroic reports of your prowess, my Lord. The virtues of Mars and the agility of Mercury will stand you in stead.'

He bowed. 'My loved lady and wife fills my veins with the fire without which even the shield of Achilles, son of fertile water, would be as straw. A thing of naught.'

'My dear Lord, the tenderness of my heart and its concern for your preservation would cry aloud to restrain you from this ordeal of iron, were it not through respect for evil omens and the knowledge that so illustrious and worthy a knight would brook no feeble woman's fears.'

He bowed even lower, knowing that he was allowing her to make no sign, to draw on no reminders of their love. From his pocket he drew a beryl, symbol of domestic concord, and slowly affixed it to her finger. 'Such graced and favouring words from the fairest of her kind lend these poor limbs armour enough, redoubled by the power of the smile from her sweet eyes.'

Then, hating himself for the reproach in her heart, he left her.

Now all was over, barren as witches. Had he really expected Rainault? Did he indeed wish to fight, had there been any true intention to fight? Was the 'real' Rainault he who would never come, the twin of treacherous Isabel? Perhaps he had known throughout that Rainault would not come: yet he had persisted in believing that he would, as he persisted against all reason in his prayers to God. Persisted too in maintaining that his father and grandfather had grown old only because they had neglected their concentration, their obsession with their own powers. Simultaneously he knew that a Name could be Named that, in this, would be fatal.

Then, in cold dismay, he realised further: felt a sensation that he had not undergone since boyhood, the fear, of which in manhood he had been incapable. That he was glad, relieved that Rainault had failed him. That he was stricken.

What was left? A renowned name, a dying House, years of caged life, and in the end, in the very end, vast unconsidered peoples closing in for the kill: all fading, corrupt, under the moon.

SEVENTEEN

A COMET had appeared, the dry star sucking up all moisture and, on the countryside it was said, all human and animal virility. Nightly it flashed, its tail streaming in Argus-splendour, its head directed towards the cold seas of the North. Peasants were grumbling bitterly, muttering that the fault was that of the accursed craven Rainault, that withered acorn, who had broken his vow and thus infected the sky.

July was reaching its peak but all things were awry. Though in summer the body had more magic the immense concentration of Duke and priest was visibly failing: life was dwindling: there would be little further year.

Other portents followed. A red cross of blood had fallen from the sky, though this was afterwards said to be the droppings of a butterfly. In a distant village a boy was stabbed for having wounded a unicorn. A dog was found hanged, perhaps for witchcraft, and near the borders a Phelia was dressed in flowers and drowned to appease . . . whom? No-one said aloud what all feared.

At Court the Countess Isabel's apartments had been completed. They remained glistening, blue, waiting, and the flowers stood rich and soundless in the tiny trellised garden. Much formal discussion was being heard about the procedure when she arrived. Should she, as a Vassal of France greet the Duchess with hand-kiss or face-kiss? Should she curtsey to the

Duke or let him first bow to her and then incline her head?

Yet the rooms were empty. The honoured carpet with its red and green blossoms, the fountain and peacock and the lady plucking cherries, vainly awaited its mistress' footsteps. For, on the last day of June everyone had stood in corners whispering tidings that the Lord of Utrecht had married the Lady of Trévers and despatched his green mistress howling, her threats and sorcery unavailing. The Viscount Charles felt particularly disgraced, and vowed revenge, his face taking on a crude subtlety. He would look up at the sky for long periods, lips moving but only his eyes speaking with yearning and hope. One day Count Benedict found him beating a row of books and the youth cried out in passion:

'They tried to kill me.'

Before the Duke could summon adequate revenge, a new letter of defiance arrived from Utrecht, rhymed, borne in by yellow heralds. The challenge was for the second time accepted, only mischance had delayed Rainault, he would come· at Michaelmas and throw defiance in the teeth of the Duke and his son.

Rainault's defection, however, despite his new vow, could not be so lightly set aside. In every College in Europe questions had been asked and suspicions aroused and, by grace of the Emperor himself, Grand Officer of the Fleece, the Archbishop was to preside at a Court of Chivalry, attended by delegates from every knightly court within range, at which the behaviour of the Prince of Utrecht would be most fully discussed.

Delegates were soon arriving. Smiling in delight,

Count Benedict moved backwards and forwards, greeting old friends. Lords from England and Scotland, experts in chivalrous procedure from Artois and Cologne, the Grand Herald, also the Lord Palatine, foremost heraldic authority in the Empire, his face diamond-shaped like an archer's quarrel, and ready to discuss a faulty adjudicature or horse's fetlock, his pursuivants armed with rolls containing all manner of precedents.

The opening concourse had been delayed for a day because of a footprint that had appeared on the ceiling. Palace poets were grandly eulogising the Duke to procure him new strength, and satirising Rainault more than ever. Simon was as tempestuous as Mars, as gallant as Count Roland, as terrible as Ajax. As for Rainault he was a barrel of malpractice, a carpet-knight, the pig's trotter that had tripped Cyprus, the false Sir Achilles who had hid amongst women. A pomegranate had been despatched to him, signifying Death.

Flavius the Nose, who had foretold Rainault's coming fall, darted about big with saws. If you watch the Yew from the East it means Death, from the West it means Life. It was possible so to enchant Brother Rainault that, on waking, he must fall in love with whatever his eyes first showed him, even if it were that toad, the Hunchback. People were calling Rainault 'Eleanor' to induce his sex to change itself. His mother was mad, his saints impure, his coinage and mail black.

'We love God,' whispered Flavius the Nose, 'so that we can be free to hate. Hate Sir Rainault.' He smiled, his face going wiled and seamy, then he jumped. 'Hate each other,' he said, pointing at a woman's scornful face,

'Love God. So as not to love each other. We are free.'

Uneasily, his listeners turned away, sweating in the heat, resuming chatter about the Court of Chivalry and, at night, gazing at the dangerous comet, wondering what was intended.

EIGHTEEN

THE Court of Chivalry, Congress Extraordinary, had
been sitting for ten days in the Proud Hall of Anjou.
The Imperial Legate presided alternately with the Archbishop, on a dais covered with crimson and purple
sarcenet and strung with many thousand of pearls and
backed by a screen of gold, against black and silver
enamelling. Hunting tapestries covered the walls, heating
the air intolerably. Candles were everywhere, to show
the presence of the Saviour: self-death leading to light,
as the priests said. Sessions, preceded by long formal
exchanges, courtesies, prayers, were lengthy, involved,
at times noisy. Arguments were produced, unrolled,
waved aloft: were challenged, refuted, amended, withdrawn, replaced, only to reappear as though they had
never been discussed. That Rainault of Utrecht had
offended against iustitia, against reason, against courtesie:
that he had maligned God, that his 'household' had
supped with the Devil: that he had grievously and
monotonously offended human dignity and seemliness:
that he should make penance, offer restitution, bare his
back, seek absolution at Rome itself for uttering false
vows, put away Isabel, give his body to the Combat,
lie in dust for three days before Duke Simon's palace to
escape the lowest circle of Hell requisite for oath-breakers.

Against this was introduced the opinion wrested from
the Universities of Paris and Utrecht together with the
Magistri Concilium of Florence, that in the original
marriage contract of Charles and Isabel there had been

that grammatical flaw, tiny, indeed almost invisible but corrosive, amounting at last to a slight and swelling, with the gibes of Time, large and impeding, a veritable insult. Further voices lumbered down the heavy stifling Hall. Was it not true that the Lord Charles had been only thirteen years of age when the betrothal was first bruited? Inauspicious, and thus voiding all subsequent proceedings? That the Lady Isabel had formerly been betrothed to Gaston of Foix and was this not tantamount to declaring that she had been already married? That though the Prince of Utrecht had not *in facto* fought at the Tournament he had *in spiritu*, and his presence was thus valid? That by reason of his grandfather's practices Duke Simon could not be considered wholly knightly, and thus oaths made to him were partially null? That, as Midsummer was the Feast of Saint John, no Christian and Son of the Virgin could fight in that season without incurring the dissatisfaction of heaven and, in intending to do so, Duke Simon had blasphemed? That Rainault displayed the Star of Saint Denis, to which he was not entitled, the quarterings of Moselle, which he had forfeited, and the Spur of Verdun, which he had stolen?

Very many resolutions were maintained. Estates were to be exchanged, golden crowns surrendered, the rights to hang banners extended, the footprints of the Duke and Prince to be crossed with copper and gold, an immense Convocation for Alarm and Mortification planned. By night the delegates flocked to balls, feasts, investitures; but throughout the day they pleaded and argued, disputing the seven meanings of 'Combat' and plotting the exact definition of 'Presently'. The Lord Estrienne's opinion was demanded as to whether any object could be considered 'real', whether anything but God existed *in toto*, and, from that, whether any man could so exist and, further, were any people except saints in natural sense 'real' at all.

In the city the lavishness of the parades and the entangled exchanges of the lords, maîtres and heralds were being watched with suspicion and at last alarm. It was generally felt that the high folk should be discussing the Comet and, though merchants and burgesses were grossing well on the trade that such gatherings always yielded, they too, excluded from the Court, mocked behind their hands, and then fell to considering the reports now hurrying in from all frontiers, and which made the papers tremble between their fingers.

Borne by an uneasy wind beneath a sky fixed and hard from which the foreboding Comet was only now vanishing, dragging after it many sighs and groans, came the messages. 'When the Plague Virgin scatters her red scarf to the winds and strokes the lips of the dying and the lattices of the living,' withered Abbot Martin read from a book newly printed in Paris, 'the world trembles, its foundations are gnawed, all is noxious and, in the upper world, the End is discussed.' In her hotel a duchess found a playing card behind her mirror and fainted.

Rumours were becoming a certainty, sixty-five trumpets sounded in unison, and the Court of Chivalry was hurriedly disbanded, announcing that it had adjourned on account of God's will and would reassemble in meet time as the Word enjoineth, directeth and prescribeth.

The cavalcades dispersed, galloping out bravely with

pennants streaming, spurs glittering, scabbards leaping in ironic sunlight, plumes dazzling, a shuffling glory of colour. But, reaching the broad fields, the pace slackened and the knights, now straggling, wondered where next to stable their horses.

In Switzerland hazel nuts had dropped from the clouds, followed by the black roses that sprouted beneath arm and groin. Led by the clergy the cantoners had maltreated their Jews for diabolical plots. A rain of snakes had fallen over Prague. Roses were spreading everywhere. The King of Portugal was already dead. In Genoa, Vienna, London the red crosses were upon the door.

In the towns of the Duchy the air thickened, as it had done when the creaking musty wings of strange birds covered them, at that former time when Plague, black giantess on a skeleton horse, reached the border, was it twenty, was it fifty years ago?

'Where Death sweeps, a man dies,' Flavius the Nose said, flapping his arms.

Count Benedict and the Lord Estrienne led the Council to beseech the Duke to leave his capital and seek refuge in the hills. He listened to the end, then explained that he would be remaining in the Palace. 'On behalf of my people,' the Duke concluded in his sombre way.

For all his dismay, elaborate and obstinate, Count Benedict was deeply gratified. The phrase pleased him. Dukes had privilege to speak thus, and privileges should be grasped manfully.

Soon the Duke was riding round the city in quarter-armour, with Lord Mayor and Provost, ordering bold

PETER VANSITTART

lecherous banners to be raised everywhere, to frighten or
abash the gaunt Maiden. Mirrors were nailed under eaves,
to appal her by the sight of her own face. Dishes of new
milk were to be left on doorsteps to suck in Plague, and
culverins were fired towards the east, at further unseen
marauders. This also served to disturb the air and prevent
the plague-fiends from collecting. Many people also
swallowed spiders as a precaution.

In the river tenements two deaths had already been
reported. A ghost had been seen in the Chevalier
Stephen's hotel, gliding through a wall, with a beckoning
movement. A Company of Fools had raced through the
streets mocking and masquerading against Death, playing
bagpipes in churchyards, feasting and yelling, as the
evening sky lay like a blighted rose and a vile stillness
was draped over the city.

On the Sunday, Duke Simon led another procession
from the Palace to the Cathedral, from the Cathedral to
the Guildhall, from thence to the city walls, where each
of the eleven gates in turn were sprinkled with holy
water, at every halt the procession kneeling in prayer,
the monks intoning, gesticulating, and whispering secrets.
The Duke alone remained silent. Hopelessly or angrily
the people were mumbling that, because of the sins of the
Popes, no man had entered Paradise for a hundred and
ninety-nine years.

Doctors were everywhere in their masks and yellow
beaks and thick musty robes, gazing about them mysteriously, and pocketing fees. Their pronouncements and
remedies were exchanged on all sides, each contradicting
or lampooning the other. No fat meat, no sleep during

162

the day, tilting and hunting forbidden, also fish: strict
continence for both sexes, each keeping to his own bed.
To induce fruitful thought and blood, poetry should be
read, treasure and fine paintings contemplated, music
played continually. 'If a man broods ill, his head breeds
scorpions,' Flavius had said and people crossed themselves, declaring his words holy. Should you dream of a
boil on your body or another's body, you should rise on
waking, lance the affected part at once and dress it with
dead toad or thrush.

Magnificence paled. Long halls of noblemen were
sickly with musk scent: heavy bowls of Frankish silver
were stationed on pedestals and filled with cloves, rose-
petals, mermaid-scales, garlic and all manner of spices.
On the Monday the Duke climbed a public pulpit and
slowly laid a hand across his fiery crown, 'on behalf of
my people'. For the peasant swinking in the field, the
priest kneeling at his altar, the scholar mocking in the
market place, the groom bending over a horse, the pallid
lawyer haggling above his thin dry papers.

Amongst themselves the higher nobles ordained that
no regard must be shown to this vicious intruder, which
must be outfaced and dismissed. They gathered for a
garden feast under the late July moon, attendants
standing in late sunlight with torches burning, to scald
the lurking Maiden.

'Man too often restricts himself by conceiving God.
It is in effect a surrender. Unless God be conceived as an
extraordinary and hitherto unexplored part of the self.'
The Lord Estrienne smiled, continuing, 'And, to return,
is it not true, Your Grace, that human energy is no longer

strong enough to fashion a God sufficient to prevent this agony?'

The Archbishop shook his grey, marbled head. 'The Illustrious has permitted himself two errors. Item, in imagining that awareness of God limits the soul of man, whereas in fact it enlarges it. Item, in envisaging God as finite and confined to that which is outside Him. As nothing is outside God the proposition lacks substance, defies reason and is absurd. The visible universe itself is but a mood of God. In addition, the manifestation of God's wrath has never been more needed than in these times of excess, indulgence and frivolity. When God withdraws His countenance, the world sinks back into the primal poison.'

A visiting prior inquired as usual how, if the world originated in poison, it could be a manifestation of God who was *in nomine* Good. The Archbishop declared patiently that, had God created the world Good, He would have limited Himself and denied life the Wonder of the Incarnation. Life falls, in order to rise higher: God dies in order to live more fully.

A voice said doubtfully, 'So the Blessed Lord's crucifixion was undergone not only for the Salvation of Man but for the benefit and improvement of God! But is it not sinful to imagine that the Almighty Father is capable of improvement?'

The Lord Estrienne, like the others refraining from wine on the advice of all physicians, drank steadily from an empty goblet, then declared that a god was neither good nor bad, but contained in himself the destructive and creative impulses that worked alternately, in the manner of a Gallic water-clock or Ruthic sewer. 'The real Fall of Man was when he became self-conscious and no longer God-conscious. Perhaps Adam was in fact the poet Lucian. It was then that man separated himself from his soul, standing midway between angel and animal, separating himself from those hidden and latent energies within him that could penetrate the seven layers of consciousness and make him first spirit, then angel, then archangel, until finally God. City-dwelling man has sacrificed his energies for the Idea. Notwithstanding, the Idea too can be used, if man steps back one pace it can be in order to go forward to the Third Heaven. To use the Idea to escape the Idea.'

'Not forward, my Lord,' the prior objected, 'neither backwards nor downwards nor upwards. Nor again does he remain static. That is the Mystery. That is the veritable Incarnation. When Man moves yet remains still. The Seven Personalities indeed clamour to be reached, and so released. In order that the total Personality can be acquired, as Jesus acquired it, and be rejoined to God the Father. Freed from frustration, by contemplating Jesus the Seven, then Man is freed from desire. Freed from desire he is no longer obsessed by and therefore dependent on Death. Then he is free to die. And, in Death . . .'

The gleaming hollow goblets were ceremoniously raised, then again laid down. Napkins passed across dry lips. From across the still, shadowy gardens, the branches and leaves at their various levels already coated with fragile moonlight, drifted plaintive music, remote, as if from across water or from the hillocks of Green Folk.

The Archbishop again shook his head. 'There is no Death. "Life Eternal" the Lord said.'

'Life Eternal is, nevertheless, distinct from eternal life.'

Another voice intervened. 'You must recall the structure of the universe, as dictated by the wisdom of God. We are taught that God is One: Life is One: the Universe is One and, by reason, One is One. But since we are beneath the sky we are so situate as to receive the dregs of the Universe. This is our Cross. Simultaneously it is, as has been mentioned, our chance of Redemption. Without God we are nothing: without God thought is emptiness. But we must distinguish between emptiness and the Void. The Void, according to the learned masters of Alexandria, creates the Blood and is therefore Fullness.'

He sat back with an air of satisfaction while the Lord Estrienne gave a short shrug. 'For myself I understand that, according to the Moorish doctors, our human brain is not yet complete. So that we are attempting absolute knowledge with an imperfect instrument. Thus all that we can hope to do is to fashion and establish a vocabulary, a pattern of words, to deepen and partially fulfil the meanings of words, to probe every possible depth of words, so that, many years later, the scholastics will have a language in which to attain ultimate perfection.'

He paused. 'I would prefer to say that it is not individual man who thinks and feels, but Life that articulates itself through Man. Thus it is without meaning to praise this man, blame that man, but rather to examine and comment on, with detachment, the movements, deviations, and after-effects of the Life that forms and maintains each, distributing energies without further plan than mere expression, variation and ultimate exhaustion.'

Beyond them, in arbours and groves, in the chapels and halls and closets, in the Duchess' apartments, the courtiers, ecclesiastics, men-at-arms, pages, maidservants stood about uneasy and waiting. Even the Wild Boars were scared, and locking himself in his room the Viscount Charles refused entrance to Young Roger. Everyone was clasping cushions stuffed with rue. Armed men stood at all gates to drive off any from the infected streets. The very friends of the Duke and Duchess found the soldiers impossible to move or bribe.

In black and scarlet, Flavius the Nose moved about quoting ancient proverbs. 'To break the Plague wear new boots until they split.' And, creeping up to a lady he clasped her from behind and whispered, 'If Plague begs for a florin, give her two and do not follow.'

Night closed down and still the lords talked together in the garden. The moon burned deeper and whiter into the sky. A bird croaked from over the water. In the Palace all were now speaking in whispers, few daring even to make a sound. A complete hush lay over the city.

At last a sudden outburst was heard, momentarily stopping and chilling the blood, so that, from various parts of the gardens, dogs began howling in unison.

The harsh noise was from the Duke's apartments. Noblemen and their ladies, servants and dwarfs, cripples and priests and soldiers looked at each other, seeking help, joined in sudden and forbidding equality. It was from the Duke himself. He was singing, unaccompanied, at first in slow hoarse tones that were gradually rising and assuming a thin, insistent power. But no-one could understand the language. It was as though an antique statue had arisen and was chanting some archaic dirge from a lost and perhaps cursed people. Even the Lord Estrienne was frowning in perplexity as the voice reached him. Not one word could be identified. The motionless hearers scarcely dared breathe. But the entire Palace was resounding: the singing was now almost a howl, joining that of the unseen and anguished dogs. From beneath peaked, jewelled caps, lofty artificial hair, feathered helms, faces met each other in terror, weeping, as the invisible Duke sang on and on, wrestling on behalf of his people.

NINETEEN

THE Duchess broke into the Duke's apartment and, so
untoward was the atmosphere, blown in from the rising
streets, that few noticed and no-one spoke.

None could for many years have seen her so roused.
Wrapped in a black simple robe, her hair untended and
unadorned, she went direct to Simon and with no more
than a perfunctory inclination caught his hand. He stared
at her, his face lustreless, worn, pulled down at the
edges, only his eyes starting to glitter. The servants fled.

'My Lord, the Devil has opened his black wings. Now
let it be our turn to assail him. Let God witness the
strength of His anointing and the powers of His regent.'

He attempted to focus her correctly. 'What is it? What
are you doing?'

There was no mortification in her voice, nor did her
spirit quail. 'Since I have no place in your bed I must seek
one in our people's hearts, as I should always have done,
under God's will.'

He watched her, morosely, jealously. 'What are you
about?' His tone had risen a note and was peevish as a
stripling's. 'The people are recognising life's folly and
falling into death. . . .'

She interrupted him, pushing his words aside with a
strength and lack of ceremony he had known and
tried to forget. 'Were Our Lady Goddess Mary to grant
me a vision, I would see you and me, my Lord, caring
for them in these our gardens. We are in the room
of God, who has called His people to follow Him, and

be as children, and who allows all children mercy and love.'

He said with tired unconcern, 'Your Grace, from the riches of your heart you speak of what you cannot know. Plague does its will. The people will die. Death will row them across. To venture among them at their last is to risk madness and endure terror. Furthermore, what you have proposed would be condemned by the Church as an attempt at self-destruction.'

She tossed it aside, her wide eyes very bright. 'For the same reason, my Lord,' she flashed at him, 'the Church condemned Tournaments and those who partake in them.'

He was about to be angry but his blood failed and he desisted. Weariness crept into him, seeking for the skeleton beneath his fine skin, to lay itself beside it. Katherine stepped slightly back.

'Look at me as I am, my Lord, not as I was. Look too at yourself, as you are, and what you are fated to be.' She came close to him again, and her voice lost its sting. She said gently, 'You have laid your curse on me because you have had your way of me and are tired of my body. But what if our souls are tired? Can you save your soul alone? Can I? Reflect, my Lord, that I, who would burn for your sake, seek my own redemption now, at this instant, in the midst of our people whom God has condemned for His secret purposes but whose brows our hands could cool. From my love and my duty to you and your high office . . .'

She ceased, momentarily paralysed as, with dignity spent, he moved back, raised an arm as if to ward off a blow, then started to shout, as though he were his own son, loosed and out of control, all decorum shattered. His face was abruptly bloodshot and angry, transported by interior flames. 'This is not your people.' Usually so calm his voice lashed all bounds. 'This is my people, suffering no other lord but me. Why do you not surrender too? A castle lowers flag, raises gate, sends out keys. I would give you all war's honours. As you once yielded your honour to my touch. But you are too strong, and that is treachery.' He grimaced wildly, leaning for an instant against the lily-painted wall, his scarlet robe now hanging over him as though all at once too big for his shrinking form. His head was shaking and averted as fever beat within him. 'You had my youth, Katherine. You saw me. Every time I thrust into you I lost more and more of myself. From our first haul together. You ambush. You infected Charles. Your blood. You swore on your heart and thigh he would get better and find grace and you swore vainly as all people do. What thoughts could you have had when I loved and filled you? When you quickened? Your pride, your pride grew poison and it touched your son and grew on him. Your goodness distracts him and his spirit hides. As I grow old . . .' He was gazing at her, but through her and but for the intensity of his body she would have turned. 'I ride to the centre with my lance maintained. Old god of stickiness and covert purposes. End at the oak do we all and need no more mirrors. Shoot at the target and reach mid-most being. Women have no centre, only vapour and dream. Sorrow a piece and the bed-fall. I cannot hear you now. Only the fearful, white faces painted on bellies. Cowardly men showing Caesar all but wounds. You trap me by my own hair and dangle on my tree. To the snake that bites its own tail.'

Gripping his head in both hands, his face now sweating, he groaned, 'You tie me to the wheel. Why cannot you give me more, more than ever you do? Strip me more utterly, touch me more deeply? Why cannot I ride beyond you and all women, press myself further and lose myself darker? If only to hell and extinction, where cities burn and the soul howls. The hisses and stews and the boiling and coiling. Is it because you have no soul, only a brazier? But she had once, did once, was once. We get lost. Was blessed Arthur a Robin, a Bear or a Raven? If then, Christ the Fish came, he did not want to come and he sends us plague. I accuse you, wife and mother, you take all hearts from me, you stir up all eyes as you stir mine . . .'

She tried to reach him and for a moment they were struggling together, in joyless and twitching dance: his chin was on her shoulder, his mouth twisting as if in prolonged attempt to bite. All colour had drained from his eyes into his face. He gasped. 'You cannot escape fire. The little dungeon-girl with the wounded cheek shelters her man from poison and there's a curse there too however the cat may jump. Though no law fits it and for you there's death or love. You must anoint my feet, not crown yourself, and I'll bruise your heel. Weep at my tomb and cleanse myself and my son and the lines from my brow, and scourge your sweet body too for invading my tower. Sunlight hides in gold-shower, but if once there were nine of you you are no sun. If I ride the night with my hunt behind me and my brother in my eye, you will have to let me be. To bow to my solitude-sun and salute my unbroken unsharable. You wept for the stag and failed my hunt. It's you who grow old. You have not crown, not cauldron, and a monster shall eat your heart too, if the dwarf slits my bag and my flame dies and I lie under hills and sleep.'

She seemed striving to prolong the dance and he swayed to and fro, sleeping on his feet, their shadows vast, mawing the narrow room, his body urging itself towards exhaustion and satiety. Yet his voice, as if sharpening itself against some invisible grindstone provided by devils, continued, shuddering while speaking, as though it would never cease.

'Why aren't you surprised at my gospel? Why don't you utter a strange sound? Out of Egypt. And I wanted you neither male nor female, clothed nor naked, virgin nor unchaste. With neither three faces nor one. Not in bed nor out of it. Never and always the same. But you want to make terms and feed thousands and reward swine. To shame me. To split my soul and eat it. To wait amongst rocks spurning all others though I sail twelve seas and suffer all trials. But I am that I am. I am I. I am I. I am I. Stuff your belly with guns but you will not tear out my other eye. The wisdom of I is eye. The people may seek you still but I am father, my hill-top is thunder and sad. Night sky is doom, and your star is under. Oniy, I cannot die, I am not mocked and whatever is done to mine and my thumb I will repay. You will not rape my people. Die for your own sins, let me avenge theirs. When I overcome death I must hunt down Jerusalem.'

She heard no more. The fever was clawing him and,

drenched, he fell over her, fumbling for her, choking, whispering that dreams were around and that they must love. But she was Duchess and guiding him, and she knew at once what she must do and who not to inform.

Plague was creeping throughout the city. Trees were parched and sickly under a curdled sky in which unusual birds seemed to hang motionless. Water in pond, canal, river was as if solid. Streets, squares, arcades appeared unpleasantly enlarged. Anguished voices whispered that the Duke himself was infected.

Daily the stones echoed with lumbering carts as the wealthier families moved out to a great camp in the hills, though the Archbishop, as he departed with his library, granted indulgences to whoever would remain. These carts, piled with furniture, window glass, strong-boxes, were followed with groans and imprecations from the mass of beggars, lepers, maimed, that had risen up, pushing in through the gates from which the guards had fled, emerging as if from under the earth, their bodies twitching and discoloured, and now haunting the fevered town.

In many streets echoed the cries of striking, bleeding flagellants singing hymns in outlandish tongues, jeering at the sacraments, chasing away priests. The tall splendours of the capital were tarnished. A mist was growing. Dogs had been hung above the death-pits to attract and consume demons. Above the stone-bellied hotel of the merchant Jacob Anvelde the Great the carved motto 'A Full Household is the delight of the Lord' faced the streets sardonically, for, within, the halls were empty, the galleries dusty, the store-rooms abandoned. In stricken households apartments rang with the rival jabberings between priest and doctors: the priests demanding extra payment, for was not such dangerous sickness the punishment for most grievous sin? The doctors meanwhile were loudly bemoaning the expenses of cordials and red curtains. Both wailed that they were risking life and soul in venturing into a house cursed by the Lord.

A belief was about that, if you found the black roses on you, you must rush to infect someone else and, thus freed from the Devil, you would be well again. The children were singing flatly in the streets:

'Maggie Plague
The black girl
With the big Arse.'

In the tenements a woman had screeched that she had seen Ahasver, the Wandering Jew, stinking like a German and sliding out to poison wells. In the body Water and Air predominated, Fire sank, dreary vapours prevailed.

Effigies of accursed Rainault were burnt in the villages, craven Rainault whose malice had caused this calamity, and pierced the Duke from behind, and, even in the Guildhalls, the lingering councils condemned that Lord Rainault before muttering about the diddling Jews. Daily the dead-numbers increased. The very clouds smelt. The beast peered from behind men's eyes, reason vanished and it was as though God had gone mad. Supplication rose to god Galen, god Avicenna, god Aesculapius. Sacred ribs of Child Hugh, of Louis the Saint, of Joanna

the Mad were borne through the city: also the hair of
Saint Hubert and the weeping image of Our Lady of
Waters. Pronouncements were issued from the University
about lancing boils, the rhymes to be uttered when laying
the toads on them, the colours of which to be thinking.
Fumes of smoking incense, myrrh, sulphur, thyme, laurel
and vine drifted against the thick, ill air upon which the
steamy sun burned incessantly. Rope was charred:
houses were hung with celandine, orange peel; angelica,
nutmegs and nettles were chewed and dancers trod their
particular steps to hypnotise and reduce sickness.

At the Palace all windows were draped with red curtains and birds flown to keep the air moving and terrify
unseen worms. Storks' nests were burnt. And still the
disputes continued. Was the Body the enemy of man, to
be scourged and thwarted and discarded? Or was it
man's instrument, to be trained, trusted, extended? Or
man's toy, to be decked but not trusted? Or, as the Lord
Estrienne suggested, none of these, but, rather, the result
of all of these? For two days the Duke was not seen and
men trembled, until the Duchess announced in state that
he had indeed had a fever but had besought God and all
was well.

The Plague had come on the ninth day of the seventh
month and in every hall voices were arguing the significance. The seventh month was that of the Conqueror,
He who Prevailed. Therefore seven was auspicious. Yet
there were also the Seven Sins. There had been the Nine
Worthies, the Nine Shining Ones, though these were
perhaps devils: also, the Nine Angels of Art, on their
mount. But, again, had not Satan the nine noxious

emanations and was not God's wrath manifest in the Nine Demons of India?

In the Palace kitchens several women were already sick and at last, from the Duke himself, now whole again, came the order for the Court to disperse to towns and castles on high places.

Ostentatiously, no-one showed haste to depart. Lords and ladies sauntered from room to room, giving orders as if in afterthought, only their eyes fugitive and agitated. The dwarfs watched them with concealed expressions, wondering about their own fate.

Many had said, though untruthfully, that Viscount Charles had already fled, enflamed by fear of losing his chance to be Duke.

At the last moment, with black and silver equipages all prepared, the Duke announced that whereas he commanded that his beloved Wife, his renowned Son, his companions, knights and officials should at once depart, he himself would not be leaving.

This provoked an immediate but ceremonious outcry. With tears in his eyes Count Benedict protested that he would not go. He was no false Peter to leave his master.

'Obedience to masters is at all times enjoined,' the Duke told him, but speaking more gently than was his habit. 'Your love and consideration do not escape me, but my service must be maintained.'

All pressed to kiss the Duke's hand. In his face some contempt lurked as he watched them bowing each other into position to take their leave.

Finally the Duchess appeared, her Ladies a few steps behind. All were in subdued dress, because of the anger in the town, even though the Duke had said that such temerity deserved the most flaunting display possible. In this, however, Katherine had gained her way and she herself was in black.

Katherine and Simon faced each other. Neither spoke. The Palace hushed as they stood, waiting as if in an effort at recognition. Then she sank slowly into the curtsey inherited from two generations of court life, and he too made his salute. Yet it was now insufficient. The years spoke. Both hesitated, meeting a verge. Katherine's blue troubled eyes crossed with the Duke's, blue against grey-green, in a further chess, seeking entry and challenging.

He too permitted trouble to shade, then seal his face. Stepping forward, very close to her, he visibly forced himself to speak, as if from a hundred miles of being.

'Lady, I crave permission to kiss your lips, for the kind and beautiful words they have always uttered.'

She had been trembling: now she was weeping. Before she could reply he laid his hand on her arm. His eyes were left steady, in possession, but his hand too had shaken. He bowed again, some part of him gainsaid: he lingered, downcast, so that no man should see his face.

Clad in gold and sable, the Duke stood in the Library, handling a treatise on falconry, while from the sickly courtyards came the last sounds of departure.

Striped and jingling, his cheeks and great nose painted blue, Flavius was beside him and now frowned disapprovingly at the lofty pillars of books, of which he had always been jealous. Eginhard's *Annals*, Suetonius' *Life of Augustus*, Joinville, a Physiologus jewelled and leathered, the satires of Marcabru and Rutebeauf, the works of Statius and the Singers of Arras. On his forehead he had bound a thick sapphire, the stone of prophecy.

Flavius had been imitating the postures of the statues ranged between the rows of vellum and parchment. Now he drank wine, having cautiously stirred it with Marengo steel and, emptying the bottle, grinned, then handed it to the Duke. His voice gasped slightly.

'Books now. They try and trap things, out of the air. Ideas, prayers and so on. They fix them tight.' He managed his high, capering laugh, and said, 'One day they will have sucked everything from the air. What then? All will be stopped. Heaven and hell will be emptied. As for kings,' he chattered on, his eyes, even brighter than usual, filling with pain, 'they used to be killed. They were surrounded and cut down with the scythes. So that the land could dance again.' Behind the blue, cumbrous nose his eyes now pried invitingly, 'The earth ages. She needs more rich bodies: to keep alive. She sighs for our great ones.'

The Duke made an impatient sign of dismissal. With dancing movement Flavius withdrew to the door, flourished a bow, then lingered. In his voice was an ambiguous intonation as though an impure pity had joined purest mockery. 'He is leaving you with the absurd and the distressed,' Flavius said, then vanished at Simon's angered exclamation.

Count Benedict, all solemnity and reproach, had already taken his leave. Now the Lord Estrienne and the Noble Friend came for their farewells. The Paymaster

General stooped over the Duke's ringed hand, his face still adroit and meditative, though he said nothing. The Chevalier embraced his master and was about to begin a speech that he had been some hours preparing but the Duke's gesture forced him to desist. The entry of the Viscount Charles made the two noblemen retreat, slowly, with many bows and protestations of eternal loyalty.

The Duke felt wearied. His son stood before him, round his neck the amulet containing fragments of a unicorn's horn. That hot blotched face under golden shoulder-length hair made the boy emissary to 'Wild Lands'. The father envied him, despised him: he loved him yet had no love for him. Standing with the fingers of Death perhaps already trained on his sex and arms, while the blackened corpses were being laid out for the carts and the heat trickled everywhere and the sun itself became discoloured, the Duke realised another thought, entering his mind like a spy. 'He is hoping that I will fall.' And remembered that night, so long ago, when he had not known whether to laugh or weep as his own father died.

The Viscount was struggling for speech. He was angry and violated but could find no words. Seeing his agony, the Duke smiled, but at this the ruined cheek darkened more than ever and, muttering incoherently, the Heir rushed from the room. 'They are coming,' he shouted, safely outside, and fled down to where the horses were waiting. There he met his mother. Hoarsely he said, 'I want to ride to the East.'

'But you can, if it pleases you.'

'I do not want to.'

He flung away, leaving Katherine alone, her ladies not daring to comfort her.

The Duke remained thinking, in the warm vaulted library so crowded with manuscript and volume, with tapestry and marbled feature, while beneath the heavy mullioned windows drifted the cries of the suffering town.

Katherine had gone. Of all his cruelties this expulsion must have been the worst. His thoughts fidgeted, hastily turned aside. Isabel too had gone, or rather, she had never been. He was at the dead bitter centre of a harsh and falling world, in which the Right Wing was crumbling and about to flee. The dance of the universe was sinking. Here was the enemy that could not be outridden, and against whom standards and eagles would not prevail. He thought of Flavius' jeering and appropriate legacy: the absurd and the distressed; and wondered whether the immensity of this suffering would avert the jealousy of God.

He raised his head. Tables, flowers, even people had other and secret faces always threatening to erupt into existence which, if not actual, was usual. People carried within them their own ghosts, their own unknowable knowledge, like that strange voice and tongue that had welled up in him as he sang for the Land's deliverance. He had been entered, possessed by the spirit that guards rulers and whose promise still makes some form out of life even if, as the Lord Estrienne maintained, as man advanceth towards God, God declineth towards man.

Perhaps women felt this, when opened by lovers or robbers.

He reflected on his surroundings that still withstood the corrosive lick of heat and sickness. All these oblique enscrolled devices; the balms, the burnt sandalwood, the saffron and snake's backbone: the Virgils and Ovids, the Augustines and Pauls. What happened when books were burnt? As perhaps a note of music still wandered in remotest sky, so might books be actually enlarged by their own ghosts. Was it they who protected him? He sighed. He was so immune: Death would shrink from him as He had always done. As He had at the rout of San Steffano when twenty knights had died at his side: at the siege of Mantes when his companions flopped down one after the other with arrows and dysentry, leaving him upright, commanding, yet queerly hopeless. He was protected, though he could distinguish, years hence, a new Duke falling headlong to the blackness, men and horses inextricably tangled, slipping on ice and blood, and bearing with them into doom the ruins of the Duchy.

He sighed again: how long it had been since his senses had spoken full-throated and his soul sang. His old terror of burning cities or of being stifled by his helmet rebuffed him less than the effortless precision and evenness in which he had moved for so many years. He had ridden as smoothly with his father over some battlefield in moonlight, with ghosts and bodies everywhere, arrows sticking in them as they lay outstretched, fixed like blanched monstrous birds silently feeding on their guts. Such a sight, from the safe side of immunity, outbid the heart, the shriek in the heart, and remained longer than any present reality. Than the signing of a treaty, a diplomatic exchange, the Game of Robin and Marion, nails left lying to trap ghosts and found dripping with blood in the morning. If only the Tournament. Attila most refreshing of comrades. And Charles charging towards you year after year, until at last you realised that a terrifying occasion was at hand, coiled up and ready to strike. Oh Isabel, fleeting and illusionary, I have lain frenzied in the night, wrapping my nakedness round a cushion, a dream, a doll, a page, aching for release.

The Duke stirred. His features, which had collapsed, gradually revived and he sat upright. How gaunt the Palace was becoming. Tapestries, chests, statues were now vast in their loneliness. The immense space between himself and the lives now gasping and struggling at their last was like the silence of fearful angels. The stillness of painted antlers, breasts, eyes was monstrous in its gigantic outcry. Giants were riding through mountains. Playing-card knaves split the sky with their grins. The armour-suits along the wall were a frontier against which the soul beat in vain, crying for a little life, a little madness. He would go on and on, untouched and untouching, to end years hence, empty, unregarded, shriven, forgiven, but nothing: in the deep fretted sepulchre of his House.

A new population was astir in the Capital: huddled beneath gabled arcades or advancing half-naked from river slums. Waiting, spare and separate, on bridges, were the Monatti, the hardened gravediggers with skulls painted on their breasts, lowest of the low, madly grabbing with thick hooks whoever they could, grunting triumphantly in their new kingdom, making abrupt merry gestures, and piling dead, dying and drunken alike on their *misere* flesh-carts. Doctors flitted by, black-robed and hooded and wearing the long yellow beaks filled with drugs. Pedlars crept from door to silent door offering snakes, bats, excrements to disquiet and rout the infected air : or the dried toads to lay on boils. Occasional wails from within mingled with the hilarity of the Monatti while, in deserted markets, the Brothers of the Free Mind danced higher and higher, sometimes fighting with bloody Flagellants and screaming that God had usurped heaven by force, fraud and injustice, and was trying to divert men's eyes from his own enormity.

From the dirty weavers' quarter Adamites were emerging, naked, many of them dancing and praying before an ox dedicated to Dauber Luke the Holy Healer. A company of feathered youths led by a Prince of Sots fled and capered about the streets, ridiculing Death and daring him to strike. Voices were intoning that now was the end of the world and the shrouding of all living. Still the sun burnt away at the thick blue sky, making everything evil and explicit: a child lying twitching in a gutter: a dead pig half-choked with cabbage and dung: an image of Saint Roch hoisted, sharp and leering, to exorcise the Maiden. More lascivious paintings were also displayed to tempt Death away, also to distract people from the agonies and disfigurements of the tainted.

In other quarters priests and people alike had flung away their clothes and were dancing mindlessly to pipe and drum and flageolet, played by figures disguised as

Death, all teeth and bone and skull, and with wooden scythes hanging from their necks. Out of a church deserted but for a solitary monk, a deep voice tolled like a bell:

'A new Commandment have I given unto you. That ye love one another.'

Meanwhile the absurd and distressed had taken possession of the Palace. As the last lordly retinue disappeared over the moat, the courtyards and banks, the steps and outer halls became crowded with poorer citizens, the guards throwing aside their halberds and joining in. The palsied old men from the market place had risen, striving to reach safety. Continually there sounded over dimmed, lost heads a shrill crow, powerful and unappeasable, issuing from the eunuch, Eneas Giorgione Cock, who stood on a throne flapping arms and throwing back his head, while to and fro strutted the dwarfs and freaks, leathery and lined, chewing plaguewort, sniffing discarded oranges that had been stuffed with aloes, hyssop, juniper, waving standards seized from walls and chapels. Jumping too, as if in a game to give energy to ghosts. In a corner a one-legged, one-armed clown was speaking, half in rhyme, to a crowd of dirty thick-eyed children.

'He can see our thought. Not to come he chose. Though his eyes close he can see in the dark. He is Rainault. Pray that he relents. For his merciful intents pray. In his hands are claws. His claws are talons. He gnaws. He flies.'

Many had been complaining that the Duke had ridden away, leaving behind only a counterfeit. Particularly prominent was Hode Hunchback, gibbering with disdain for that cowardly Flavius who had rushed to hide his head in safety.

Grinning venomously at a mute who had been born without ears he exclaimed in an unusual voice, 'Hateful toady. His nose, stuffed with beetles. But I have a holy name. My lovers can call me Muot.' At which several jeered and he repeated furiously, his small black eyes flaring, 'I have a holy name. When I wear my broad-brimmed hat my two ravens tell me what is about. I have hung for nine years on an oak. I can give you all maundy. Call me Muot and I will cut you down.'

Soon all were fighting together for food, sitting or squatting on the long tables clumsily erected in the Banqueting Hall of the Fleece under the immense eyes of tapestried heroes. Wine flowed. Quarrelling, chattering, munching, the dwarfs clambered over the serving-girls, thrusting at their sex, were parried and driven off with obscene jests or submitted to in wild insensate laughter. The eunuch, indefatigable, driven by incessant personal compulsion, still crowed and the soldiers, many silent as if shamed, drank deeper. Bodies kept tiring and falling inert across the table before gradually recovering, hands lurching for wine. They were far from angels. Many of the beggars that had appeared had never been in the Palace: throughout their thin lives they had been watching it with parched and aching eyes: and now they continually left their stools to paw at armour, tapestry, silver ewers, or to make water over the floor, pleased with themselves, and feeling ennobled.

Giant musty tuns had been dragged from the cellars

and broached, with crazed figures stumbling towards them cursing the Death outside, threatening Him-Her should he intrude, making ferocious and incomprehensible taunts and at times parodying the priests. Despite the aromatics the air had a dry persistent smell, like soot, and above the crowding din a voice hissed wretchedly:
'Lepers are coming.'

As yet there was no stealing. Most still knew that if you carried a stolen prize across a Duke's threshold you would be blind for the rest of your life and, afterwards, burn.

The hands of the heavy painted clock above the arras had been destroyed by the dwarfs, who now stumbled across the floor screeching that they had thus prevented the sun from setting and that joys would be prolonged. Several girls had already been stripped and a few remaining musicians, not yet soggy, were playing some weak tune. But suddenly the eunuch crowed again, higher and more urgently, and then silence slowly gathered, pushing through small unsteady groups, and over the many straggling figures heaped at the table. The dwarfs recoiled, the cripples dragged themselves up onto their stumps, the girls covered their loins. Hode stood mouth open, features unprepared.

Looking up, all saw a resplendent image. A live sheet of gold transfixed in rubied light: emerald sleeves airy and puffed as dreams; sheaves of crimson: long pale hands fiery with riches: a blue and green hat coiled and crusted with diamond and gold tissue.

The Duke was framed between Messer Florio's black carved arches. Faces, peaked and scared, stared back,

feeding on him, grasping his outlines, groping towards
reality. A woman's frightened voice whispered, 'But
where is the real one? It is devil. Trap. A trap. They have
it so.'

Others murmured, 'They have it so,' and stepped back,
several crossed themselves, another voice muttered, 'The
accursed. Dagon.' A legless man spat derisively, moving
to one side on his hands. His companions belched. A
blind beggar, scarred and pitted, mumbled, 'The real
one, eh! Silks and finery they say. In a golden mountain.
In the south. Gold. And what's that?'

They could not believe in the erect, motionless Duke.
Here was the counterfeit, the illusion. But, guardedly, on
hands and knees, Hode was creeping towards him pointing a stick as though it were an arquebus. Still the Duke
did not move: he might have been a wooden decorated
emblem or stock, a figure stuck in the arch to receive
devotion or obloquy, to bear sins or stand while a
ruined Caesar sought renewal.

Already Hode had reached him, had measured: then
suddenly, as the tattered groups watched, suspended, the
hunchback jabbed at him, at his sides and feet and at once
sprang up, waving, setting off the shrill cock-crow as he
cried, 'It is the Duke. The Duke.'

The hour was Mercury, the Duke's hour. Slowly,
childishly they crowded to him, having first held up a
mirror to further reassure themselves by seeing that it
would carry his reflection. The stunted and twisted, the
malformed and disregarded; the man with three ears, the
mouthless girl, the mutes and the handless, the blind and
unwitted, they crawled and hobbled, limped and felt

their paths to him, drawing together to receive his touch, to feel his glitter, waiting with rare and ecstatic excitement until he should speak.

At the back, several crippled men and their women, linking themselves to remain upright, were quietly waiting their turn. One bearded old fellow in sacking tugged at the others, his voice hoarse and thrilling:

'Do you see, brothers? He has tears. Tears in his own eyes. For us. Our Duke!'

The merchants who had remained arrived at the Palace in deputation, to discuss with the Duke measures for the protection of the city, forming indeed a new Council. Up the Palace steps they now walked, treading with roused yet slightly rebellious curiosity the wide steps, eying the massive sculptured foliage, keeping apart from each other and heavily protected by hyssop sponges, fumigatory braziers, red banners and pigs' bladders soaked in gall.

When it was known that the lords had fled, many of the more substantial burghers had returned, half-ashamed of their previous impulse, half-proud of their present daring. A new resolution was in their mien and, as they crossed the many-hued apartments of the Duke's stronghold, they continued to tread as if with premonition of coming powers which they were as yet unable to name.

The city seemed more enlarged than ever, gaunter, and in the streets, the flitting faces of passers-by were as if the dark pinched features of woodcuts had assumed life, yet a life of less vigour, less future than that which they had now renounced. A priest stood quite alone before the Hôtel de Ville, unmoving, like a dark misshapen plant

on a brooding evening before thunder. Many sufferers
had been laid out to die in the Field of Mars under the
splendid canopies, standards, pavilions erected for the
Tournament which, as the blackened bodies still gasped
and twitched, cursing priest and family for having
abandoned them and recoiling from the hooks of the
naked smiling Monatti, filled their last thoughts of a
powerful invincible Rainault, fanged and glistening,
scything where he listed.

The usual clatter of horses, the submerged roar of
crowds, the ponderous bells and singing trumpets, the
beat of armed men and the multitudinous cries and threats
from markets had dwindled to a child's hollow whisper
or an unfinished and blasphemous rhyme. 'Dirty Death,
let God stew . . .' and the soft lubricant sounds of young
Flagellants sinning more in order to have the most to
repent and thus mount deeper into heaven. And hopeless
women searching for their children and moving gro-
pingly, weirdly, as if striving to advance through miles
of invisible water. Several men had been stripped and
strangled for having been christened Rainault.

Silences were broken by the grind of tumbrils, the
occasional dirge for the dying, the sudden wail. People
moved on tiptoe, lest Death should notice them. On
islands in the river, spires, turrets, battlements thrust up
to sickening heights. In an almost derelict tannery a
father who had lost mother, wife and children in a single
night, all infected by a lonely and jealous neighbour who
had seen no reason to depart to the underworld unaccompanied, muttered that the penalty was now being
paid for hearing the infernal drum which had ushered in

the wicked embassy from Utrecht that fatal Easter so many thousands of years ago. Now was it abundantly clear that Christ had been crucified in Utrecht and that it would have done His heart good to have heard of Duke Simon's victory.

Circles had been drawn on streets in which to entrap Death. In some quarters, arts and vanities and jewels were being hurled into fires. Many gypsies had appeared, moaning, yet behind their noisy grief were sly cutting smiles. Jews were cursed but without vigour from the enfeebled mass of surviving bodies which, pierced by the evil, unremitting sunlight, prayed, indulged in grotesque and lopsided dancing, copulated on streets with whoever passed, flung away badges and trademarks, stole and plundered, or lay down quietly on pallets waiting for Death to stretch out his hand and choose them. On some altars brothers and sisters had been allowed to couple, as a precaution against the Maiden. Jasper reached high prices, Plague fearing it. More dark birds gathered in the sky. And from the loftiest pulpit in the Cathedral a lawyer was shouting in satisfied tones, his eyes two flaring lights splashed on a darkened pitiless face.

'When ye therefore shall see the abomination of desolation spoken of by Daniel the Prophet, stand in the holy place, then let them which be in Judaea flee into the mountains. For wheresoever the carcass is, there will the eagles be gathered together. Then two shall be in the field: the one shall be taken, the other left. Two women shall be grinding at the mill: the one shall be taken and the other left.'

Gesticulating, his voice echoing down the deserted

aisles, he shouted to the shadowed, appalled city, 'The Lord of that servant shall come in a day when he looketh not for him, and in an hour that he is not aware of, and shall cut him asunder, and appoint his portion with the hypocrites: there shall be weeping and gnashing of teeth.'

The Duke sat with his burghers registering the edicts. Several University Magisters and doctors of the Hospital of Saint James' Mercy had been with them, advising on measures with which to fight the Plague. Only the crabbed features of Jew Plate had survived in misty Perilous under the John of Gaunt Bell. Laboriously he copied down edicts about diet, salted water, the curing of fish, the disposal of bodies by fire despite objections from the few Cathedral canons that remained: edicts about isolation, inspection and the demolishment of many buildings. Latest returns showed that deaths had lessened during the last three days. Prayers were to be quickened, for a change of weather.

All windows in Perilous were open, the sunlight flaming against the red draperies. A pause had succeeded the Duke's short speech of thanks to his advisers. The merchants and doctors, still slightly awkward in these surroundings, nevertheless smiled slowly at each other. From the interior and from the courtyards came laughter, curses, songs from the many hundreds camping there, in sanctuary.

From the passage sounded firm iron steps and a mutter of voices. The Duke, on his throne apart from the round crowded table, looked up, a sudden raised gaze of anxiety shading his smooth features. The others straightened themselves and, as the doors swung open, they saw, in full armour, his grey head tired and heavy above the black and gold plating, Count Benedict, distinct and odd against the rich cloth of the burghers.

Breaking all commands, defying the new conception of 'treason' that against all opposition the Duke's father had made the hard pole of public affairs, he had returned without permission, unable to absent himself from his master any longer. He stood, head bowed in untoward humility, one hand trembling.

'My Lord Duke . . .'

But the Duke had already risen and advanced towards him, breaking all precedent. He extended his hand to be kissed, then opened arms to embrace the old man. The advisers hurriedly withdrew, not wholly pleased with this disturbing of their small reign.

'My Lord Benedict,' the Duke said finally, 'you have indeed answered our summons promptly, and you have our grace.'

It was not to be thought of that the Count's disobedience could be admitted between them. From that day, nevertheless, in penance for deserting the Duke, for obeying him in the nominal but not in the real sense, the Count condemned himself to eat black bread for a year and lie on a bed only twice in a week. During the following days he never left the Duke's side : long steamy days could not exhaust him nor infinite labours break his spirit.

Early each morning the Duke left the Palace, garbed like a penitent monk and discarding almost all ceremonial, retaining only a coronet and followed by the one page he had let remain. Those around him as he descended to the town, those who saw him in the streets bending over the sick, ordering the total destruction of an entire street, over-ruling landlords and guildmasters with subtle interior laughter, chasing away or killing extortioners who had been demanding a man's house, wife, daughter in return for a thrush to apply to the sexual parts, or who watched him contracting for supplies or reorganising the markets, noted the new gleam in his cheeks, his unwonted energies and curiosity, his fits of anger, sarcasm, impatience, contempt that broke through the features that had been passive for so many years: the strange flexibility of their lord, now kneeling over a dying weaver, flaying a reluctant householder, comforting an orphaned child with words precise yet intimate, climbing a tower to polish a tocsin bell that had rusted, the bell that was to announce the cleansing of the Square of Saint John. They noted the extraordinary appearance of satisfaction with which he rode back at nightfall, shaking with weariness yet with mouth and eyes firm, even exultant. Hitherto he had been seen only stiff on horseback, motionless in a litter, remote at banquets, horizontal on a brocade couch or in hierophantic isolation at the High Altar.

There assembled about him during that last blackened week the atmosphere of those stories about his grandfather. How shepherds had worshipped him in fields: how he had strangled two snakes sent by the jealous Virgin when he was only two hours old: how he had slain the cattle of the sun. Awed, people whispered that Simon had kissed a dead ravaged man, who had instantly taken up his bed and walked.

As for the Duke himself, he found that he had no time to sing silently of 'Wild Lands' before the day hobbled to its end and he dropped, disarrayed and finished, to his bed, contenting himself with a little fruit that Hode brought him, and the ironed wine he shared with his page and Count Benedict. He had set himself to overcome this dark and bleeding Maenad and he must succeed. The population of dreams had invaded him: nakedness everywhere and the faceless leper and the tall man with tiny hands, claiming possession. In new irony he wondered whether this were the real Tournament that had been intended for him. By God or his blood or his desires that were so secret that he did not himself know them. Quickly he shied, not caring to renew that desolation when his spirit had tired, aged and quailed before the expectation of fierce Rainault.

Increasingly, he overtook himself considering Katherine. Once, in the bed, she had said, 'I believe, my Lord, I believe that there is nothing that you cannot win. Nothing that you cannot do. But let me help you. Because in all honour I know you.'

This knowledge of him he had admitted and at once resented without caring to know why. It had been a complex form of treason. Now, however, in this solitary, hurrying existence in which he was encamped he felt, obscurely, glad of it. Armoured. Should he indeed send for her, or would her actual presence reduce the image that had been forming in him?

Did she too cling to that green moment of the past, fondling it like a jewel, holding it to holy light, checking herself from raving?

'There will be less kneeling,' he once said aloud but when Count Benedict asked his meaning he could not explain.

The Duke with his merchants, magisters, and dominies and loveless around him fought his campaign in the beleaguered city, which now seemed to exist only in his will, the wharves, warehouses, towers, walls, squares, arcades, porticoes shrinking into his palm while he considered decisions. He fought until the late August day when, feigning a limp and with one eye covered, watched by many thousands of silenced, quivering citizens, he drew a golden circle round a high marble slab and, with loud but controlled tone, commanded Death to step into it.

TWENTY

THE Plague abated as some of the heat left the sky. Death was caught in the circle and must again be subject to fate and God's will. The soul was re-established. The dark tide of human dross sank back to whatever swamp it had come from. Caesar's month had ended.

On their return, the lords and courtiers found to their dismay that the Duke was withdrawn and ungracious as though, while he had himself demanded it, he was reproaching them for their defection. Such were the ways of Dukes.

Rejoicings rang through the capital. Golliads danced in the guildhalls: golden bulls spouted wine: simnel bread was handed on civic plate to excited mobs. A Wild Man was seen and chased. Commendations from the Archbishop followed thanks to God from the Chapters. Proclamations were issued, immense beacons lit, and drunkenness was general. The return of the Duchess through rose-arches entwined with S and K in reds and whites aroused full-throated acclamation, though no-one had yet ascertained how it was between her and the Duke.

The matter of the Michaelmas Combat had not been forgotten: indeed, anticipations were now strengthened, for whereas before the Blackness people had expected little more than the splendour of a victorious passage of arms, now they dreamed of a glory less articulate but akin to anthems, out of the soul.

The Field had survived the short deadly madness of the Plague. Flags still lay scorched and burnished in the sunlight. Carpenters were repairing the stands and painters decorating them: more flag-poles were being hammered into the earth. The Lady lay in her pavilion fondling the Unicorn, though no Isabel would come in this life and no eyes now penetrated the desolate richness of her apartments. And the Viscount still bedded alone, or with Young Roger.

The year was decaying: Lammas had passed and despite Flavius' prophecy the Prince of Utrecht still lived. With tempered humours you could overcome the decisions of stars and only the Duke could close that hectic career. 'Our Duke will scourge him for breeding the Plague Bitch,' people said.

Yet it could not be felt that the Duke was now behaving in a way fitting his knightly vows. It was rather disgraceful, many thought. Weavers were making money, mules were packed with full burdens, ships sailed again with laden holds, the burghers paraded squares and terraces and avenues with insufferable satisfaction, but at court the noblemen lowered their voices. It was as though the Duke had shifted his name-star. No longer did he exercise in the yard with Angevin Henry under Count Benedict's strict eye. Instead, he spent many hours alone, the pages said, reading: or gazing from windows or busying himself with those pushing merchants: the mill-owners, loom-owners, clothiers and Florentines, equipped with the sinewy and dangerous techniques of the Lord Estrienne. He passed much time inspecting and praising a novel loom brought from Brabant, that could do ten men's day-work in an hour. Frequently too he rode out to watch the clearing of various tenements,

Plague's bed he maintained, careless of whatever the priests might declare, with their talk of God's wrath. Careless too of the liberties of those he dispossessed, his soldiers driving them away, however much they wailed and cursed.

At talk of God's wrath the Duke exclaimed indignantly. Were God so petty he was no God, or was too old, or too young, or a cheese-god of no account. God was necessary only because of the Fall, as a check to Reason. But suppose there had been no Fall? Could it not be true, he suggested, sitting once more with Chaplain Van Meeg over wine, that God had indeed died on the Cross and that only His ghost now haunted the universe, whining and ineffective, sufficient to trouble the conscience but yielding no consolation?

The Chaplain giggled, in imitation of the Chevalier Stephen and replied that, though the proposition was not without Grammar, it contained three separate heresies.

The Duke's neglect of his Court and of his military ardours provoked considerable frowns, though preparations were mounting daily. On all sides there gathered a conviction that the Combat would not take place. Disappointment in Palace arbours was echoed in tavern bowers, even amongst vine-dressers and peasants tramping in from over the river.

Count Benedict then pointed out that the first five letters of each of the protagonists' names contained two vowels. Did this balance indicate that no solution was to be expected? Or a sympathy innate between Prince and Duke so that fighting would be unnatural, Tyr-like, almost incestuous? Priests saw a swallow fighting an

199

osprey: the Prior of Saint Faith dreamed of the Virgin assaulted by the Ram, Rainault's protecting spirit. As the likelihood of actual combat appeared to recede, there grew throughout the Duchy a dream of two gigantic shapes, equal in grandeur and skill, meeting on spiked horses in tumult and shock in a vague space as if above clouds, the universe holding its breath, and then rocking with the impact so that the sun shuddered. In victory must be the culmination of life, like the song maintained between planet and planet: like a dance, the ending of which would induce a fifth season, a fifth monarchy, a unique life.

TWENTY-ONE

BOTH sun and moon were glittering at either end of the sky, illuminating the gods as they stood erect on pedestals as if awaiting a summons from the ultimate cloud of the universe: yellow Apollo, black Saturn, green Venus. Beneath them, pools, rocks, grottoes, caverns lay in careful disorder while the centaurs slept and Orpheus played, and the nymphs twined and postured with their shepherds.

The dancing was over but the music persisted, a ducatia, the lute gliding within and beyond the unseen virginals and pipes, vielles and rebecs, always about to withdraw, hesitating, as if afraid of its own tender climax, falling silent to rest in echo, then recovering, gathering strength, finding the path, weaving in and out of the sunlight scattered between the leaves.

The masques had been arranged by the Architect General to celebrate the rout of the Plague. The courtiers sat in glistening groups, listening, eating subtleties shaped into phoenixes, griffins, pegasi, lifting their glasses to be refilled without turning their eyes from the actors, the lofty head-dresses of the women making a jumble of tints even above the knotted, emblazoned caps of their lords.

In rose-pink Brussels tulle, the Duchess sat on a silver chair backed and shaded with silks of Gentiana-blue. Count Benedict and her Chancellor stood on either side of her and, at her feet on a stool, was her youngest and favourite countess. In repose Katherine looked older, lightly mocked by the cutting sunlight. Listening with closed eyes she saw thin figures moving soundlessly just before her and, simultaneously, centuries away; Hermes the Cursed, Prince of Thieves: Our Lady of Crossways; a princess who pricked her finger; a boy whispering a Dawn-poem; finally, riding towards her from distant lands, the man who had once been very young and who had never ceased to haunt her, and to whom she gave all thought, all love, whatever his inclinations.

Standing exactly midway between Duke and Duchess the Chevalier Stephen was still watching the dancing that had vanished. A riddle was unfolding: 'Only by the dance shall ye achieve stillness,' though some line about a circle still eluded him. In a deeper part of his dream hung Bellerophon, blind and damned, and mountains seen through mist, and a face in a fire, and fragments of all the random Good Hours: the pause in the hunt for wine, a sight of girls stripping in summer, lying beneath trees reading Master Villon or Master Luigi. Hearing this clear silvery music you reached the soul, that land above the moon, the celestial chord suspended for Christ the Dancer. Even the sun halts to hear the song of the phoenix as it prepares for death. Then the soul acquires sufficient silence to hear its own song. That antique and dwindling soul, if it were true that before the Fall red Adam could hear the music of the planets. At such a time a daisy blocked the sky, a tower could be hidden by a leaf, a fountain be but sound, and jewels soft as ash. Stand, and in rarest stillness hear that inherent music of which this long, visible sweetness is the merest echo.

The Archbishop kept a little apart, the Cardinal-Legate sleeping on his left, Van Meeg sipping pleasantly on his right. La Borde's face was slightly marred, slightly stained, as if over a faulty translation from Lucan and he heard no music. Whensoever it had come, the Plague had taught a coherent lesson. For the wise all is for the best, and disaster but quickens those parts of life hitherto inactive. The Parable of the Talents, whoever had said it, was justified: use not only the pawns: Plague, like defeat, summons the kings in all men to confront God and Devil. As old Venantus said, naught but the deeds of just men survive in a flower that is blessed: sweetness comes from the grave where the virtuous lies dead. Such language was the real music, supreme fount of the spirit, ichor of angels.

The assembled Court saw nymphs and shepherds regather: out of the pools rose rocks, sirens: a ship's mast was briefly seen, passing through flittering green shadows towards fair havens. David was singing to dead, mutilated Jonathan, broken in Gilboa's dust.

> 'Low in thy grave with thee,
> Happy to lie.'

All recognised the words of old Abelard, wafted on an artificial breeze as the ship passed and the sirens waved and languished.

> 'Since there's no greater thing left Love to do;
> And to live after thee
> Is but to die,
> For with but half a soul, what can Life do?'

The girl at the Duchess' feet had lifted her head, opening

large intent eyes, feeling Katherine's knees against her and telling herself that, for love of her Lady, she would gladly renounce and die.

> 'Peace, oh my stricken lute,
> Thy strings are sleeping,
> Would that my heart could still
> Its bitter weeping.'

Here, in many-hued flutter, like the opening of a vague and illusionary fan, birds were being released from peach-trees, from the outstretched hands of the gods, from caverns: blue birds, red birds, birds all golden, swarming above the watchers: red and black beaks, green heads, red eyes, blue wings tufted with mauve or gilt, legs hung with bells: all soaring above peaceful heads and vanishing.

The music strengthened as the masque faded, building up its ceaseless analogies within Count Benedict's old mind. Music has colour, this lowering melody was purple, the Duke's colour, but the Duke was also Jupiter who needed blue: on his shield, however, was the black of prudence and the vert of joy: and the Duke was not only Duke but a man who had once been a boy scared of Count Benedict's flashing shield. And now the music was again shifting into yellow, though the yellow Apollo on his marble made no movement and, simultaneously, the melody was white, if pagan yellow and Christ purity could be thus combined. How extraordinary it all was. Contradictions abounded. Everywhere Rainault was coming, was not coming: the Lord of Peace had brought a cutting sword: the Lord of All had died at the hands of petty scoundrels.

Looking about him Count Benedict felt tired, unpleasant, too old. Then he wondered whether colour continued to exist in the dark. Or, when a red cloud drifts into blue sky and turns yellow, what happens to the original red. As the music softened, however, his speculations mouldered away into old tales. Prince Conrad hopping on one leg before Jews to raise ducats for his crusade: old Raymond of Nicosia insisting on sleeping in a manger on Christmas Eve. He knew too that, locked in dungeons, were tunes of such sweetness that they drew men's souls from their bodies and, when the music faded, the souls drifted away and were lost for ever.

He sat up, blinking and discontented. This play was tedious, and furthermore, it was dangerous to linger too long in gardens.

The Lord Estrienne did not care for music: it escaped, even mocked him by its freedoms: its boundaries, what might even be called its mystery, continually deceived. It aggrieved him that musicians, by general consent the most unlearned, sottish and witless of creatures, also undisciplined, could create such binding illusions.

He had, however, been considering the mummers. How even these clowns could control the wise. Given Right Knowledge a fool could become Saviour, could overcome God. Even the clacking priests had their formulae, dry residue of lost wisdom: by the masses of Saint Sécaire and the Holy Spirit they dragged God into their clumsy hands. The question was not of discovering truth but of knowing truth. All religion was a misunderstanding, a mistranslation of Names. To make peace with God was to adjust your being to the angles of life. Call the vital principle Mithra, Adon, Dionysius, Christ, and what a tangle of illusions and conflicting imageries obscure the Name! Call one mood God and another, Devil: call authority Father, and Creation, Son. Call self-understanding 'Heaven' and despair 'Hell': confuse self-control with immortality, poetry with prayer: call the dark dream-stuff Devil and the light intelligence God, and see what fetters you cast for yourselves. Old Ficino had married Christ, Lord of the Net to Virgin-born Plato, which showed his crassness. Perhaps this little Duke was a worthier pupil: not armour, not fortresses, but precision made man invulnerable. Fix the exact name to a mood, a treaty, a Cathedral, a golden salt-cellar, a prayer, a negotiation and, given strength to bear it, you root yourself in total life, steal the Olympian fire, win the laurel, enter paradise, assume God. And despite Averroes, despite Thomas, despite goaty old Anselm, the body would answer all questions and name all names. From senses came mind, and, if there were soul, it was mind redoubled, senses at full strength, and let doubters read that sensible volume of Alexander of Aphrodisias. Life was a dream: a few men knew this but fewer would speak of it or name it. The shining Tournament concealed the mouth of Hell: the savage Plague was the way to Heaven. Like the figures in the Forest Painting a thing is, is not, then is again. No man can sustain names for long, so he cries aloud for Simon the Strong, Katherine the Kindly One, and for False Rainault. The Universe stands on elephant Force, which stands on tortoise Contemplation, which stands on fire Penetration, amid the gyrations of atoms.

Smiling craftily, the Lord Estrienne hitched his dark robe a little higher. Alone of them all, he realised that Rainault of Utrecht had indeed come to this city and that no-one else, except perhaps the Duke, in his groping yet not wholly contemptible way, would ever know it.

For the Viscount Charles, sitting more golden than ever and grumbling with his companions, the music was too slow. He waited for the flute to quicken, the trumpet to charge, all to gather and break through and conquer ... but here the thought faltered, retreated, finally cowered: the tune itself was on the verge of dissolution and, through a bloody mist, the boy Charles could only sense that he and the Wild Boars were skewered on a dead field amongst famished ravaging dogs and peasants.

The Duke was alert. As he listened to the lament and cries of the viols, flutes, horns he felt himself a mass of fragments, a cloud mass deflected by winds, sundered by tempest, reassembled large and powerful, floating above the world, never finally anchored. He had plunged into nightmare but, unlike 'Robert' he had come back. In that tortured acreage of Plague he had encountered a novel and complete satisfaction as he struggled. With those unexpected people at his side it was as though he had entered a foreign country, yet which was unmistakably his own. Another and less fleeting Tournament. In the world.

How this music mingled past and present and displayed the paradox, the fool of time. That two men might be enemies to the death: the Lords Alexander and Darius, Hector and Achilles, Henry Short-Cloak and his tantrumy Archbishop: yet, with the intervention of Time are seen, years later, as sworn allies against a third, the mocker, doubter, destroyer. The seven deadly sins might in Time become the seven virtues as once they were. The reality of an object, a crusade, a Duchy, depended not on itself, for nothing remained constant, but the Time in which it was plotted.

Music made all so clear: the invisible and unspoken shone as brilliantly as stones in moonlight.

Yet he sighed, as though he had failed to reclaim his favourite hawk. So often had he wanted to relax in the peace of Nothingness: in the hunt, or in a hermit's cell, or in storming towards 'Wild Lands', or in music. Old ambitions had been ruby-hard: to lead a crusade, sail to the Indies, build a library greater than San Marco, dissolve himself in an Isabel and renew his House and his Soul. Now the ruby was being crushed and again he asked himself whether Isabel had ever existed. Was it conceivable that she was still somewhere, searching a mirror, watching the moon, fearing seas, receiving compliments from that gross hog Rainault? Perhaps Rainault was already dead, or was indeed riding towards him greedy for spoils. But no more than a spear was needed to dispose of swillpots.

The Duke smiled to himself, then felt his cheek flush as he netted a glance sent to Katherine by the young Count of Flanders. He swiftly cooled but the displeasing sensation remained and, worn by the ravages of the last month, he found that, as if surreptitiously, he was staring more and more at the Duchess as she sat, quiet and thoughtful, sunk in the music-dream.

Cornerstone of heaven, the moon was hardening. Dusk was at hand, Saturn's Hour. The Court watched the last

Masque. From sunset emerged blue Jupiter, lowered to earth on a burning planet amid White Stags, roses and beautiful boys. From the moon was Diana, in saffron, the Duchess' colour. Three naked goddesses greeted the Sire, piped by a shepherd and receiving apples from a masked Dominique. Snow now fell, changing to petals as it reached the grass. From their cave Courtesy and Mercy, surrounded by an immense scarlet butterfly, tribute to the Mother, bowed to the Huntress who inclined towards Katherine. Old Age was expelled with howls and trumpet calls. Unicorns aloft on an artificial hill were dripping roses, like Messer Leonardo's lion that had dropped languid lilies from its breast. Now the stage was crowded with satyrs, green fauns, water-goddesses white and twinkling, flying from a creaking dangerous Monster-Ram from Utrecht, soon to be transfixed by a stage-duke riding from the west, his path lit by fire with heavy purple bunches of grapes waved alternate with torches. As the spear descended, from the wrecked monster emerged a Rainault and a Turkish squire, to be mercilessly gripped by an armed statue and bundled off to Hell. Then lights flared on all sides, creating a sparkling motley of the Duke with Stag, distributing the pale blue of Peace, before an angel descended to crown him and the entire rout broke into praise.

Spontaneously, the Court, led by Duke and Duchess, began dancing, and the Chevalier Stephen, hand in that of his favourite page, had his riddle solved, for if all men danced and sang in true measure the world would be merged in the true circle of God, would clap its hands and vanish.

TWENTY-TWO

SUMMER was reaching its last glories: September, the Wind-Month, glowed deep: Michaelmas was on the horizon. For many weeks no rain had fallen and, on hillsides, by the river, in wide glistening fields stretching towards castles, monasteries, sentinel towers, the corn stood hard and dry and about to fail. In villages men stood looking at the sky and grumbling that the sun was angry because there had been failure at Midsummer: also betrayal: and the Duke had not felled his man.

Continually the peasants shot arrows into the air and hopefully watched them fall into short showers. Still no rain came. Images of the Virgin were carried through the fields. Ancient statues were drenched from buckets. Boys were whipped, their cries filled the air and their tears dropped, beseeching the stormcloud. Why did not the Duke of his bounty produce rain that his people might live?

In the Capital, however, men did not cease to cheer Simon, trade continued as ever, and the thick corded bales were despatched daily to Antwerp, to Jutland, to Norwich.

At Court the Duke had remained in his apartments for some days receiving nobody. It was said that he was silent, heavy with thought, and avoiding the Duchess.

The name-day of the Duke's father was celebrated, there was an injunction to refrain from laughter and many leant against the vermilioned walls pretending to be weeping.

Throughout were busy preparations for the Michaelmas Tournament: again the knights were arriving even
more resplendent and heavy than before: more elaborate
costumes were being ordered, anthems composed, procedure rehearsed, conferences arranged to discuss precedence: only that excitement amongst the women
stirred up before Midsummer was lacking.

The high folk moved about unsmiling, for deviation
from life's rules was not permitted, but amongst the
lesser inhabitants of the Household considerable hatreds
still persisted, left over from the events of the Plague,
and it was generally agreed that, in particular, the scourge
should be taken to Flavius the Nose.

Flavius strutted across the Blue ante-chamber and
encountered Hode, who did not move from his path.
Much whispering could be heard, behind screens,
tapestries, pillars. Seeing the hot determined hunchback,
Flavius frowned importantly, then waved his thin wand,
the bells jingling on his sleeve.

'Move,' Flavius said.

Hode, after so many years, at last stood his ground,
facing him. His features, scraped and raw, had unaccus-
tomed strength. He had a sacred name. 'The Duke and
I . . .' he was now wont to say, referring to the Plague
days. He now said wheezily, peering forward, his hump
looming up behind him with all its stars and flounces:

'You fishmonger, you bawd, you baker's toad, you
chitterling, you sleeper, you whatsoever!'

Flavius flushed, and saw that dwarfs were now
crouching at the silken entrances and blocking them. He
spat, though his glances beneath the pearled, striped cap

were uneasy. 'You litter of air . . . may the Devil drink
out of your eye!'

An instant's hush. Amongst the dwarfs and freaks,
swaying, mouthing, gesticulating, was an unsteady
baboon carrying a wicker shield and wearing a lady's
pearled cap. Flavius made to move aside but wherever he
stood Hode had jumped there before him, grinning and
taunting, 'Cullion. Pole-cat. Filth.'

Flavius' breath was coming in short hissing gasps. He
could see that a negro had entered, dragging two latrine
poles which Hode and Master Egyptian quickly trussed
together, their mouths malevolent. Panting, Flavius
attempted a little run, desperate, beating the air, but was
immediately seized, strapped to the cross, hoisted aloft,
gagged, then paraded throughout the Minions' Tower,
pelted by scullions and wenches, clawed at by the
lurching chattering baboon, finally left almost naked in
the sallow sunlight above the middens. A considerable
and raucous crowd remained for the rest of the day
mocking the crucified fellow, Hode leaping and twirling
and allowing almost everyone to call him Muot, until,
after Vespers, drawn by the tumult, the Duchess appeared.

Very calmly yet very firmly Katherine ordered him to
be released and, when they seemed to be fumbling, cut
the first bond herself, exclaiming with sudden feeling
that she would not have it so. That people should be
ashamed of their cruelty whatever their station. The
sadness and brightness in her eyes frightened them and
they hurriedly slashed the remaining cords, silently, then
darted away lest she should see more of them that night.

Riots occurred on the parched countryside, more anger was raised against the Duke followed by several gibbetings on orders from castles. Finally, as the drought worsened, affecting even the river and canals, the Church interposed, and the Archbishop and Cardinal-Legate rode side by side, in grand state to the Cathedral.

That night the clouds darkened from the west and the rain fell, at first quietly, testingly, then with more confidence, eventually lashing cobbles, turrets, fields with triumphant impunity. All rejoiced, the priests nodded amongst themselves, reserving their further knowledge and Flavius safely emerged, in fresh green and white stripes, his nose newly painted. Watching the rain, keeping close to various lords and now protected by a dagger, he capered with delight, showing his scars and bruises. 'It is expedient,' his voice was hoarse but resonant, 'that he should suffer for people,' adding with a wink and a finger to his nose, 'by his sufferings he induced God. He got you all wet.'

For three days the rain fell, fitfully, washing and blessing the gold piled in the fields.

A scrivener, writing in a solitary turret, declared that he had witnessed a marvel. A dog had howled at the moon, then in sudden fervour scratched a hole. Water bubbled up and there, before his muzzle, was the moon, fallen to earth and floating. Frantically the dog had drunk, the moon vanished as the hole emptied and, clouds darkening the sky, the animal lay down quietly, to sleep, glad of the moon in his stomach.

News arrived, confirmed by pilgrims and pedlars as well as by emissaries from Mark courts, that Rainault, many weeks back, had departed for Syria, taking Isabel with him.

He had fled. Triumph was signal, complete. Belfries were soon hammered by paeans clashing and throbbing. Men dressed as birds were whirling on poles.

Michaelmas would come and go but no Ganelon-false Rainault would uncover his shield. Some said that he had avoided the Road because of a ghost that was there. He was pox-ridden, his mother was a scullery-wench, a baker's chit, his father a base pantler. From all parts of the Duchy silver trumpets proclaimed his discomfiture, also gratitude to the Duke for having risked his person to save the people from the horrors of war.

A full Mass was sung in thankfulness for the preservation of the Duchy from Isabel's green, evil powers. The Sword of State, the Lord of the World was carried through the streets on its samite cushion to lie all night on the High Altar in the Cathedral.

On Michaelmas Day the Palace was crowded with delegates, Colleges of Arms, Brotherhoods, Chapters and Orders assembled to congratulate the Duke on his victory. The air was made lax and flimsy by brocades, satins, sleeves as the ladies carrying lemons streamed to kiss his hand, then was hardened again as massive iron lords moved ponderously forwards. The Chevalier Stephen, Noble Friend, prolonger of conferences, a tight knot of white and purple plumes in his casque, had sung a song of Amfos, King of Aragon, then a verse of Gaubertz, 'Courtly are thy Words and Days.' In the Hall of Peers, now lined with damask and golden statuary, the Duke in full armour, holding a gold and ivory sword, stood visored and invisible to receive acclamation. Masked squires with high lances were grouped behind him. The Archbishop in shining vestments was above them on the Staircase, talking either to himself or God. Voices were praising the Duke as Scipio, Count of Africa, as Alexander of Babylon, as Prince Fortune. In a separate Hall the merchants, gowned, bellied as forts, had already bowed as low as they were able. The black metallic image before them was a monster, a figuration, an emblem of past confusion, but to-morrow the Duke would be back again and receive them too. The Artois contract must be discussed, and the purchase of Elmont, and the matter of a Loan on terms more far-reaching than those of malicious Italy.

Shocked at their intrusion on such a day Count Benedict ushered them away. Things were more extraordinary than ever. Then he passed within to assist in the presentations and ceremonies and praises due to the victorious Duke. Already the Lord Estrienne, a gold chain over his black, was proffering a jewelled casket.

'My Lord Duke, at your God-given and ordained victory over false Rainault, the faint-hearted and fallen renew their hopes and give thanks.'

Such sentiments the Count heard with approval. Also the mounting piles of gifts requisite for the Victor, Champion of Lists. A thousand tuns of Gascon wine: two splinters of the True Cross: sixty mirrors fashioned by the most elegant and celebrated Venetian craftsmen: a tooth of Saint James the Less: books and parchments: bags of gold: tapestries from Orvieto: nine hundred bales of Flemish cloth: seven suits of gold tissue: fifty-eight

Spanish jennets: eleven Arabian mares: two hundred Rhenish ponies: a thousand larks bottled in Moselle: fourteen caskets of jewels: a mace studded with emerald lions: artillery: a roll of new canzone from the Master Musicians of Laon: a rhinoceros from the Lords of Sicily: a bowl of jacinths to dispel melancholy: the skeleton of a basilisk: cases of Frisian robes: hounds from Aquitaine and mules from Navarre: a phoenix calendar: a silver hippogriff with wings of amethyst and pearl: a pot of dragon's blood: linen bags of Arabian cassia: twelve rolls of silk in lilac, purple and scarlet: and an alabaster chalice containing a phial in which was secreted one drop from the Saviour's blessed veins.

TWENTY-THREE

HARVEST had been eared, the Corn-Neck been cried in the fields and already the peasants were foretelling winter's prospects by the tints of stubble-goose flesh. At night a vast moon hung over the Duchy, exploring all corners and boundaries, allowing the flesh no ease.

In the late afternoon, returning from the Court of Requests, Duke Simon had paused, alone with a hound, in the long verge between the Minor Tilt-Yard and the Vault of Shields. A new row of guns had been ranked and he stood as if holding communion with the gleaming enscrolled barrels.

Christendom was on the verge of new loves, new sounds, new treasons, new distances: these guns would speak and, like the Crucified, draw all men after them. Duke Simon was no bookless lackland, no Blessed Francis despiser of learning. Kings were at hand so great that the eye could not comprehend them, and the mind struggled to include them. The Duchy itself would burn with even more splendour and, staring at his life-hand, Simon reminded himself that he had many years to live. Years of checks and balances: glazing and mining associations threatening the ancient guilds of wool and cloth: the Jews: the English. Capet and Habsburg in their ceaseless game . . . and he gazed reflectively at the guns that in their silence claimed to solve all problems. Those virgin slender limbs tempted, he wanted to stroke, to kiss them, and there rose up in him love for his son, Charles, dreaming of attack, dedicated to the Charge, the son whom he had, more than once, contemplated killing.

The Charge would come: and one day, centuries hence, immediately before Judgment, strange figures would break into a hillside and discover royal figures in a tomb: a moment of robed, shining magnificence, then, with fearful alacrity, all would fall soundlessly to dust, shivered by light.

The Duke roused himself and turned away. He bent to touch the patient dog: he had read that in the ancient days, in the Garden, men and animals had conversed together, as Grandfather had still done with birds. All passes. And for to-night revels were planned.

The Chevalier had been singing his favourite song:

> 'It is for youth, youth only,
> To love, be loved again,
> For Beauty mocks at old men,
> The old are full of pain.
>   Aves nunc in silva canunt.'

Leaves were brown in gardens: in little drifting clusters they sank to earth. Suppose one wave of the darkening river deliberately drew itself up and defied the current: that would be the banner of 'Wild Lands', or rather, they were yet to come and he would not meet them.

In an age without miracle there might have to be less music, fewer secrets. Questions would always abound. But it was no longer 'Where shall I go?' but 'Where am I already?' A new maxim must be learnt: *Tournaments no longer take place.* The inevitable pressure of Time on events makes all things obsolete at the very instant of their perfection, saving only songs and rulers.

He was not as young as he had liked to suppose. He sighed, then drew a deep breath. He would fight no more with Charles, despite his abiding and remaining strength. 'For the sake of my House.' Charles might yet be saved.

Meanwhile, there was, after all, the necessity for Dukes. Pope, Emperor, God Himself had had limits set to their power. God, indeed, must be weakening, for at Creation He had begun that which visibly had become too powerful for Him. During the Plague the chess-men had taught their master that God was now strong only in the perfection of His popes and kings, His dukes and lords, His thralls and bondsmen. Christ had been Lord of the Seasons, the year was strengthened by the blood of gods and lords. Dukes too were powerful only in the strength of their subjects. Only those who could toughen their souls would survive and, though this was probably Christ's teaching too, the Lord Estrienne would agree.

Perhaps it was also true that, sorrowed by Time, God had become more evil than good, must be soothed and improved, at the last replaced by a more lasting perfection. That God was created daily and simultaneously had to be fulfilled, as the Lord Estrienne maintained, could not be admitted without offending the Archbishop, who had declared that this was the veriest nonsense and superstition.

Walking down the avenue towards the Arch of Rome the Duke sighed again. Not much God. No Isabel. No return to waters and green, sunlight and bare girl. He was no longer vital enough to remain alone, escape from Time and Place even in the giant delusions of warrior and poet. Still more magnificence was needed, more Blue in the palace, even though scoffers might say that lords now existed only for the pleasure of their people. Mirrors could not replace life, but magnificence could succeed natural frontiers. Katherine had known. But, having stared Time in the face, and now that her own beauty too was about to fail, he no longer resented that she knew so much.

A boy no more, no more the supple warrior that he had been, he was not yet dead. Christ the Unicorn had not yet drawn close to him. He must gather within himself more and more Duke-hood, to help God by enlarging man's spirit: use that Magus part of him to build the land against coming storms when all manner of dance should be licensed, and the World and ether fall awry. To linger before mirrors with their subtle and compromising hints was a temptation to be resisted.

He was now walking more briskly, under the yellowed leaves, greeting the archer-guards that had filed out from the Palace steps between the towering marble urns and shields and monsters and hard clustered grapes. Even an ageing Duke still had everyday works to perform as best he might.

Tree-planting had to be finished at Saint Magnus, the Trade Negotiation with the East English be reconsidered, a formal debate be heard at the University concerning the nature of the universe, twenty-one propositions, though some wished them to be reduced to twelve, in honour of the Apostles. A chess-champion was expected from Lombardy. And was there connection between leprosy and bad fish? Also, the eerie fascination of playing cards to be examined more carefully. The Viscount Charles must be found another bride, Young Roger being, presumably, insufficiently fertile. The Lord Estrienne had plans for a new university in the Northern Provinces, which must be induced to pay for it. A campaign might be needed against the Turk, in the spring. Within Time and Space, if there was no freedom there was at least room to deploy forces, though various people were saying everywhere that the earth would turn but a few years more, that the curse of Cyrus of Babylon might be fulfilled. This life was, conceivably, the real world, and, anyway, it was pleasant to behave as if it were.

Simon was mounting the steps, his head raised and stiff. He walked slowly, reminding himself that he was old and must confess that he needed support. He passed a statue of himself: perhaps this stone was now more truly 'he' than his living body, and would lie in the earth for centuries, to rise again and be worshipped and procure miracles and stories for people as yet nameless.

Quickly, and again, he was thinking of Katherine, as he had often done since that solemn moment during the Plague. To come to terms with Katherine, to transform once more the 'I' into the 'We' would be to adjust himself to himself and thus remain even with life. He would offer sacrifice to Five, Hymen's badge, the Number of Marriage, and build three altars, according to custom, and send a prayer to Alcmena-Mary, Lover of heroes.

Greeted in the State Hall by a vice-chamberlain he ordered an escort to accompany him to the Duchess' apartments. Sudden terror gripped many. To the wonder of the Court, however, he remained there several hours, supping with her alone until, as the torches flamed, the dancers in the Hall of Paladins, looking up at the sennet, saw their Duke and Duchess hand in hand, descending the Staircase, Katherine with flowers in her hair that were understood to have been plucked by Simon himself.

It was the Feast of All Souls, honouring the Dead. Lord Baldur was in his grave, honoured in a thousand households by red and purple flowers: Polly the Sun-god too had dropped his head: the leaves were falling as the year rotted away. October had come, month of Vintage.

In the Mars Field the Tournament hangings had not yet been dismantled. The lists had faded, stained by October rains, flags hung sodden and discoloured, ragged by last week's gales, then already beginning to recover as the wind rose, blowing bitter into the grass, itself empty and tousled. The Lady had vanished, the Fountain was dry, the Pavilion held itself precariously against weather. The Tournament had cloyed and gone dead.

Through the dilapidated scene a boy was wandering, gathering sticks under an immense hooded sky. Clouds were dark and hard, like broken ominous statuary. He was frightened, and crossed himself because of the Dead. Old Arthur, the autumn wind, was filled with dying souls who shrieked as the tempest swept to earth, and he must be careful to keep his mouth shut, for only this morning mother had said that you risk your soul if you address a ghost first.

As he watched the wasted lists an expression of sorrow touched his face. Then he chose his largest stick and began prancing backwards and forwards, lunging, stabbing, covering. He was the Duke, overthrowing

enemies. Then, bundling up his gatherings, he hurried forward in relief.

Soon the sun had gone and the night was roaring. Voices gabbled in taverns.

'There, our Duke, descendant of Charlemagne, he broke the false heart . . . Rainault was it, or Otto? Forced him off. We'll see no more of him, the evil one. He never gave away a boot in all his life. Praise to our noble, thrice-blessed and orthodox Duke, for having borne our sins.'

All Souls Night. In castles they would be plunging into old Tom Maccaber's Dance of Death. In cellars alchemists were mumbling over their cocks' eggs. On the country-side man-wolves would be about. Here in the flamey streets gangs of shouting youths rushed everywhere, burning effigies of a devil called Rainault and the pest witch Isabel and driving ghosts away with clubs. Children called hoarsely to Lighthouse Mary. Caps and scarves were bunched and twisted into secret signs. Forges were white and deserted. In the Jews' Market a very old man was offering to sell his shadow. By Saint James' manger a fight was raging between disguised gods and animals. Once the Wild Hunt swarmed past, scattering the crowds and led by Hellekin, Herodias, and Salome, haunted by the Baptist's head. Down shadowy alleys beldames were mumbling about fees due to the Three Crones, One Bed, Woollen Bed and Many Beds, and that devils were compounded of the stuff of the moon. Quaking voices told that in the Cathedral wandered Wode, he of the Hood. Shouts rose above the clamour from tumbledown taverns. Those with keen sight and clear souls could already see the Dead crossing the landscape and carrying their lanterns. Blessed Katherine, hear us.

Despite everything, however, all was more orderly than usual. To-morrow the Duke was to wash the feet of thirteen beggars, and what woman would not desire to anoint him with spikenard?

In his cell old Abbot Martin, having seen the lanterns of the dead, heard the wails and cries from the street, sat back contentedly. A few more sinful generations and then the Third Year would end, the sixth thousand year of the Holy Ghost, and, as the sun for the last time set in praise of the Trinity, the very stones of cities would dance.

Soon he was asleep, for he could not now be expected to know that a new feeling was abroad, rumour's son: that, by achieving his conquest over the infamous Ram, the Duke, Victor, all shining and ever young, had overcome Death, and that he would redeem all men, even though their souls were haggard and their dispositions worse.

ALSO BY THE SAME AUTHOR
The Death of Robin Hood   4031